MUHAMMAD ALI
Fighting as a Conscientious Objector

REBELS WITH A CAUSE

MUHAMMAD ALI
Fighting as a Conscientious Objector

John Micklos Jr.

Enslow Publishing
101 W. 23rd Street
Suite 240
New York, NY 10011
USA
enslow.com

Published in 2018 by Enslow Publishing, LLC.
101 W. 23rd Street, Suite 240, New York, NY 10011

Copyright © 2018 by John Micklos Jr.
Additional materials copyright © 2018 by Enslow Publishing, LLC.
All rights reserved.

No part of this book may be reproduced by any means without the written permission of the publisher.

Library of Congress Cataloging-in-Publication Data

Names: Micklos, John, author.
Title: Muhammad Ali : fighting as a conscientious objector / by John Micklos, Jr.
Description: New York : Enslow Publishing, 2018. | Series: Rebels with a Cause | Includes bibliographical references and index. | Audience: Grades: 7-12.
Identifiers: LCCN 2017030323 | ISBN 9780766092563 (library bound) | ISBN 9780766095533 (paperback)
Subjects: LCSH: Ali, Muhammad, 1942-2016—Juvenile literature. | Boxers (Sports)—United States—Biography—Juvenile literature. | Political activists—United States—Biography—Juvenile literature.
Classification: LCC GV1132.A4 G74 2018 | DDC 796.83092 [B]—dc23
LC record available at https://lccn.loc.gov/2017030323

Printed in China

To Our Readers: We have done our best to make sure all website addresses in this book were active and appropriate when we went to press. However, the author and the publisher have no control over and assume no liability for the material available on those websites or on any websites they may link to. Any comments or suggestions can be sent by email to customerservice@enslow.com.

Portions of this book originally appeared in *Muhammad Ali: "I Am the Greatest"* by John Micklos Jr.

Photo Credits: Cover, p. 3 CBS Photo Archive/Getty Images; p. 7 Robert Abbott Sengstacke/Archive Photos/Getty Images; p. 9 David Fenton/Archive Photos/Getty Images; pp. 12, 21, 36, 43, 48, 52, 60, 68 Bettmann/Getty Images; p. 17 Pictorial Press Ltd/Alamy Stock Photo; p. 22 Central Press/Hulton Archive/Getty Images; pp. 26, 33, 73 © AP Images; p. 39 Express/Archive Photos/Getty Images; p. 46 Rex Features/AP Images; p. 57 AF archive/Alamy Stock Photo; p. 63 The Ring Magazine/Getty Images; p. 76 Frank Tewksbury/Hulton Archive/Getty Images; p. 81 Francoise De Mulder/Roger Viollet/Getty Images; p. 84 Ray McManus/Sportsfile/Getty Images; p. 89 MCT/Tribune News Service/Getty Images; p. 93 Anadolu Agency/Getty Images; interior pages graphic element Eky Studio/Shutterstock.com.

Contents

Introduction 6
1 The Beginning of a Legend 11
2 Golden Boy 20
3 The Greatest 30
4 The Legend Grows 38
5 Living in Exile 47
6 Epic Battles 59
7 Falling Star 72
8 The Legend Lives On 80

Conclusion 92
Chronology 95
Chapter Notes 99
Glossary 108
Further Reading 110
Index 111

INTRODUCTION

Known worldwide for his brash boasts and stinging punch, heavyweight boxing champion Muhammad Ali became an American rebel for saying nothing. Reporting for induction into the US armed forces on April 28, 1967, Ali refused to respond when his name was called. Instead, he presented a written statement: "I refuse to be inducted into the armed forces of the United States because I claim to be exempt as a minister of the religion of Islam."[1]

With that simple refusal, twenty-five-year-old Muhammad Ali chose to give up his heavyweight title and millions of dollars in potential earnings to stand up for his beliefs. By taking on the United States government over this issue, he even faced going to prison. His protest against serving in the Vietnam War came at a time when most of the American public still supported the nation's involvement there.

The United States wanted to prevent the pro-American government of South Vietnam from being taken over by

Introduction

When Muhammad Ali (*front, second from left*) refused to be drafted by the United States Army, he was supported by numerous fellow African American athletes.

the communist regime that ruled North Vietnam. By 1967, some 400,000 American troops were already stationed in Vietnam. And now Ali was refusing to join them.

Ali already served as a lightning rod for controversy. Many people admired his wit and flamboyant style. Others thought he was boastful and arrogant. His conversion to the Muslim religion in 1964, when he changed his name from Cassius Clay to Muhammad Ali, caused further controversy.

During the civil rights movement in the 1960s, the United States struggled with how to fully and equally integrate African Americans into the nation's economic, political, and social structure. Meanwhile, the Nation of Islam—or Black Muslims, as they were also called—believed in opposing white oppression by whatever means necessary, including violence. This frightened many whites. It also disturbed some African American leaders, including the Reverend Dr. Martin Luther King Jr., who advocated nonviolent action to gain equal rights for blacks.

Ali's refusal to be drafted caused a tidal wave of reaction. Not only was he one of the most famous people in the United States, but his stand also had political, racial, and religious undertones. It led to nationwide discussion of all of these issues.

For refusing to enter the US Army, Ali was sentenced to five years in prison and fined $10,000. He remained free while his lawyers appealed the case. However, he was stripped of his heavyweight title and his boxing license was revoked.

Ali did not fight for three and a half years. Those years, when he was in his late twenties, mark the prime of most fighters' careers. "We never saw him at his

Introduction

Ali and members of the Black Panthers marched through New York City in September 1970 to protest Ali's conviction of draft evasion. The conviction was later overturned in 1971.

peak," his trainer, Angelo Dundee, said years later. "If he'd continued getting better at the rate he was going, God only knows how great he would have been."[2] He also lost millions of dollars he could have earned from boxing during that period.

A remarkable thing happened while his case worked its way through the courts. As casualties mounted in Vietnam, the tide of public opinion gradually began to turn against the war. Many people who had at first disagreed with Ali's refusal to be drafted now supported him. They applauded him for risking his career and his fortune to speak out against what more and more people were coming to believe was an unjust war. "During his exile," wrote biographer Thomas Hauser, "Muhammad

Ali grew larger than sports. He became a political and social force."[3]

Finally, on June 28, 1971, more than four years after Ali had refused to be inducted into the Army, the US Supreme Court voted to reverse his conviction. This further raised his status as a hero for many people. Ali was much more modest, saying, "All I did was stand up for what I believed."[4]

1
The Beginning of a Legend

Many famous people have turning points in their lives—when events lead them down a road that sets the tone for everything that follows. For Muhammad Ali, that event came at age twelve when his bike was stolen. Looking for a police officer to report the crime, he found his way into a community center where Officer Joe Martin ran a boxing gym. And the rest is history.

But long before the stolen bike, his world was shaped by discrimination. The memories of that discrimination stuck with him throughout his life. "Whites Only." "No Coloreds Allowed." Signs such as this were common throughout Louisville, Kentucky, in the early 1940s. Like many cities in the southern United States in those days, Louisville was segregated by race. Blacks lived in one section of town. Whites lived in another. They rarely interacted on a personal level. Blacks could only drink from certain water fountains. They could only use certain restrooms. They were denied access to many restaurants.

Meanwhile, World War II had raged throughout much of the world since 1939. The United States entered the conflict following the Japanese attack on the naval base at Pearl Harbor, Hawaii, on December 7, 1941. The fighting continued until Germany and Japan surrendered in 1945.

Muhammad Ali: Fighting as a Conscientious Objector

At twelve years old, Muhammad Ali was then known by his birth name of Cassius Clay. Ali began boxing after his bike was stolen, and the sport soon took him around the world as a championship fighter.

This was the world into which Cassius Marcellus Clay Jr. was born on January 17, 1942. His father, Cassius Sr., was a sign painter. His mother, Odessa, added to the family's income by cleaning and cooking for white households across town. Both of his parents were keenly aware of political and racial issues.

The war ended when Cassius was three, so it did not really affect him. The segregation and discrimination he experienced while growing up, however, shaped many of his lifelong beliefs. It bothered him, even as a young child, to see that blacks were not allowed into many stores and offices. "What did they do with the colored people?" he would ask his mother.[1] At the time, most people used the terms "colored" or "Negro" to refer to

A LEGEND LEARNS TO SPEAK

Ali's mother recalled, "We called Muhammad 'GG' when he was born because—you know how babies jabber at the side of their crib—he used to say 'gee, gee, gee, gee.'"[2] Though it would be a little more than a decade before Ali got his hands on his first pair of boxing gloves, when he finally did, he joked that his baby gibberish had actually been his attempt at saying "Golden Gloves."

black people. The term African American did not come into use until much later.

According to his mother, Cassius walked and talked early. He was never still, and he walked on tiptoes all the time. When his younger brother, Rudolph, was born, Cassius acted as the protective big brother. If his mother tried to spank Rudolph, Cassius would grab him and say, "Don't you hit my baby."[3]

Odessa Clay took the boys to church every Sunday. She taught them to treat everyone kindly regardless of their race. Years later, Muhammad Ali said this about his mother: "She's a sweet, fat, wonderful woman, who loves to cook, eat, make clothes, and be with family … There's no one who's been better to me in my whole life."[4]

Around the neighborhood, Cassius played touch football. He was so fast that no one could tag him, recalled his brother. Cassius also played an odd game. He asked Rudy to throw rocks at him. "He thought I was crazy, but no matter how many he threw, he could never hit me," Cassius said. "I was too fast. I was running left, and right, ducking, dodging, and jumping out of the way."[5] Years later, he would put those evasive maneuvers to good use in the boxing ring.

Troubled Times

In some ways, the Clays were a close, loving family, but they faced their share of troubles, too. Cassius Clay Sr. sometimes drank too much and became violent. On three occasions, his wife called the police for protection. Over the years, he was arrested several times. But he proudly noted that he never spent one night in jail.

The Beginning of a Legend

Cassius Clay Sr. also sometimes saw other women. This greatly angered his wife and years later led to their divorce.

In 1954, at age twelve, Cassius received a new red-and-white Schwinn bike. It was his first new bike, and he was very proud of it. One day in October, he and a friend rode to the Louisville Home Show. There they browsed the exhibits and enjoyed the free food.

When Cassius went outside after the event, someone had stolen his bike. Cassius was very upset. His family could not afford to replace the bike.

Cassius looked for a police officer so that he could report the theft. He found one at the Columbia Gym nearby. Officer Joe Martin ran a boxing club there. Martin later recalled the event this way: "One night this kid came downstairs, and he was crying. Somebody had stolen his new bicycle … He was only twelve years old then, and he was gonna whup whoever stole it. And I brought up the subject, I said, 'Well, you better learn how to fight before you start challenging people that you're gonna whup.'"[6]

From that moment on, young Cassius was hooked on boxing. He spent all his spare time training. "I was the first one in the gym, and the last to leave. I trained six days a week."[7]

"My bike got stolen and I started boxing, and it was like God telling me that boxing was my responsibility," he later said. "God made us all, but some of us are made special … When God blesses you to have more than others, you have a responsibility to use it right."[8]

After just six weeks of training, eighty-nine-pound Cassius made his boxing debut. Before the fight, Cassius was nervous. His opponent, Ronnie O'Keefe, was a little older and a little bigger. But Cassius won a three-round split decision.

Did Martin know then he was training a person who would one day become one of the greatest heavyweight boxers of all time? Hardly. "I guess I've taught a thousand boys to box, or at least tried to teach them," Martin later recalled. "Cassius Clay, when he first began coming around, looked no better or worse than the majority."[9]

Within a year, however, Martin noticed that Cassius had a lot of potential. He already had the speed that would later become his trademark. He also possessed plenty of determination. "He was a kid willing to make the sacrifices necessary to achieve something worthwhile in sports," Martin said. "He was easily the hardest worker of any kid I ever taught."[10]

He was also one of the biggest eaters, which helped him grow from a skinny kid into a heavyweight. Martin noted that "he would eat enough food for three or four other boys."[11]

Early on, Cassius hoped to make a living through boxing. "When I started boxing, all I really wanted was someday to buy my mother and father a house and own a nice big car for myself," he later recalled.[12]

Getting Knocked Down

Still, his path wasn't easy. One day an amateur named Willy Moran knocked Cassius out cold. But it didn't bother Cassius. The next day he was back working with Moran again.

Clay also showed at an early age the smart mouth that would later earn him the nickname "the Louisville Lip." "Almost from my first fights, I'd mouth off to anybody who

The Beginning of a Legend

Ali kisses his mother in front of his childhood home in Louisville, Kentucky, in 1965 while his father, Cassius, and brother, Rudolph, look on from the front steps.

would listen about what I was going to do to whoever I was going to fight," he said. "People would go out of their way to come and see, hoping I would get beat."¹³

While Cassius excelled in the ring, he struggled at school. Years later he realized that he had dyslexia, a condition that causes people to have difficulty reading. Often it causes them to see certain letters reversed. Cassius also struggled to solve math problems. He barely managed to graduate high school. He ranked 376th out of a graduating class of 391.

Indeed, some of Cassius's teachers thought he should not graduate at all. Principal Atwood Wilson stood up for him, however. "One day our greatest claim to fame is going to be that we knew Cassius Clay or taught him," Wilson said. "He's not going to fail in my school. I'm going to say 'I taught him!'"[14]

Part of the problem was that Cassius was acutely aware of the prejudice against blacks throughout American society. He realized the odds he faced in trying to succeed in a world controlled by whites. He saw black people with high school diplomas and college degrees hanging out on street corners because they could not find jobs.

"I started boxing because I thought this was the fastest way for a black person to make it in this country," he said. "If he's good enough he makes more money than ballplayers make all their lives."[15]

FEAR OF FLYING

Cassius Clay almost didn't make it to Rome for the Olympics. After suffering through a rough airplane ride to one of his amateur fights, he feared flying. At first he thought he might not make the trip to Rome. Finally, his father and coach persuaded him to go. In the end, he made the trip and won the gold medal. "If I had not faced that fear and gone on to win the gold medal at the Olympics, I might not have become the heavyweight champion of the world," Cassius later said. "If I let fear stand in my way, I would never have accomplished anything important in my life."[16]

Cassius fought more than one hundred amateur bouts, losing only a handful of times. Along the way, he won two Golden Gloves championships and two national Amateur Athletic Union (AAU) titles.

One of his opponents was Jimmy Ellis. They split two close fights and became friends. "Ali spent all his time in the gym," Ellis said. "That's where he lived. He wanted to box and he wanted to be great, and that's what his life was all about."[17]

In 1960, Cassius won the Olympic trials in the light heavyweight division. This gave him the chance to travel to Rome, Italy, to participate in the Olympics. Cassius looked forward to proving himself against boxers from around the world.

> **"I started boxing because I thought this was the fastest way for a black person to make it in this country."** —*Muhammad Ali*

Sports Illustrated said he had the best chance of any American for a gold medal in boxing. The magazine also noted, "Clay likes to display supreme confidence by doing intricate dance steps between passages of boxing."[18]

Soon Cassius Clay would get to display his boxing talent on a worldwide stage.

2
Golden Boy

The Olympics offered Clay a chance to showcase his boxing skills—and his vibrant personality—on a worldwide stage. He took full advantage of the opportunity. He quickly demonstrated that he was one of a kind.

Once in Rome, Clay soon established himself as the "young clown prince of world athletes." He joked with other athletes, shaking hands and telling stories.[1]

"One of my teammates told me that if I had been running for mayor of the Olympic Village, I would have won the election," Clay later recalled.[2]

Clay had such fun mingling with the other athletes in Rome that his coaches were concerned he might lose his focus. Still, Clay trained hard. He ran two miles early each morning. He worked out in the afternoon. "He worked for that gold medal," said teammate Wilbert "Skeeter" McClure. "He was one of the hardest trainers I'd ever seen."[3]

Clay won three fights to reach the gold-medal bout. There he defeated Polish fighter Zbigniew Pietrzykowski, a three-time European champion, for the light heavyweight title. After two close rounds, Clay pummeled his opponent with combinations of punches in the final round and won a unanimous decision.

Young Ali is in the ring at the 1960 Olympics in Rome. Ali defeated Soviet boxer Gennady Schatkov during this fight and moved on to the next round.

After the bout, Clay stood solemnly on the medal stand and accepted his gold medal. The next morning he paraded around the Olympic Village, wearing the medal.

A Russian reporter asked Clay how it felt to win a gold medal for a country that wouldn't allow him to eat in many restaurants. Clay replied, "You tell your readers we got qualified people workin' on that, and I ain't too worried about the outcome. The USA is still the best country in the world."[4]

Punching Up

Winning the Olympic gold marked a fitting culmination to Clay's amateur career. "That was my last amateur fight," he announced after the bout. "I'm turning pro."[5]

A large crowd gathered for Clay's triumphant return to Louisville after the Olympics. There he recited the first of the many poems he would later become famous for. In this poem, he described how he triumphed in Rome just like Cassius from the days of the Roman Empire.[6]

Ali won the Olympic gold medal for light heavyweight fighting at the 1960 Games in Rome. Here he's shown surrounded by the event's silver and bronze medalists.

Despite being an Olympic hero, Clay still faced prejudice. One day he and a friend went into a restaurant in downtown Louisville. The waitress told them that the restaurant did not serve Negroes. Clay had his gold medal draped around his neck. He politely explained that he was an Olympic champion. The two still had to leave.

"I wanted to tell them all that they should be ashamed," Clay later recalled. "I wanted to tell them that this was supposed to be the land of the free. I had won the gold medal for America, but I still couldn't eat in this restaurant in my hometown."[7]

The next big step for Clay was finding the right people to manage his career and promote his fights.

Initially, Clay was managed by the Louisville Sponsoring Group, a group of eleven wealthy white men. Together, they pooled about thirty thousand dollars to launch Clay's career. Clay received a ten-thousand-dollar signing bonus and a guaranteed salary of $333 per month, which would be deducted from his earnings. Earnings would be split fifty-fifty for the first four years and sixty-forty in Clay's favor after that.[8]

Clay used some of his signing bonus to buy a used Cadillac for his parents. He also set aside some money to pay taxes.[9]

On October 29, 1960, just three days after signing the contract, Clay had his first professional fight in Louisville's Freedom Hall. His opponent was Tunney Hunsaker, a part-time boxer from West Virginia who had a record of 17–8. Clay won an easy six-round decision.

Looking back later, Hunsaker said, "I'm honored, highly honored, to have been the first person Muhammad Ali fought in his professional career."[10]

MISSING MEDAL

Even after winning the Olympic gold medal, Cassius Clay faced discrimination. He was refused service in restaurants. Some white people threatened him. In his autobiography, *The Greatest*, he described being threatened by a white motorcycle gang leader who demanded that Clay give him the gold medal. Clay refused. He saved the medal, but he was so disgusted by that experience and the prejudice he faced that he said he threw the medal off a bridge into a river. Some people believe the medal was simply lost. They think he told the story to make his point about how evil prejudice is.

Years later, Clay sent Hunsaker an autographed photo. It said, "You gave me my first fight as a professional. Thank you and may God always bless you."[11]

Soon after his first fight, Bill Faversham of the Louisville Sponsoring Group sent Clay to California to train with Archie Moore. He thought the young boxer needed more professional training. Moore was the light heavyweight championship of the world.

Moore tried to teach Clay how to fight up close and how to punch more effectively. But Clay didn't always listen. He had great confidence in his abilities. "He thought he would never have to do any in-fighting because he was gonna be so swift and always out of range, etc.," Moore later recalled. "It was useless arguing with him."[12]

After only three weeks, both teacher and student agreed it would be best if Clay went back home. "To tell you the truth, the boy needed a good spanking," Moore later said, "but I wasn't sure who could give it to him."[13]

The Louisville Sponsoring Group searched for a new trainer for Clay. In December 1960, they went to Miami, Florida, to interview Angelo Dundee, who trained a number of fighters. They offered Dundee a choice of a guaranteed salary of $125 a week or 10 percent of Clay's earnings. Unsure of Clay's potential, Dundee took the salary. Over the years, that decision could have cost him a fortune. Fortunately for him, he and Clay's sponsors later worked out a percentage deal.[14]

Eager to start training, Clay left for Miami right away. He began training with Dundee on December 19, 1960. The two would work together for twenty years.

Dundee helped Clay hone his awesome physical gifts. Clay stood six-foot-three and had very long arms. In most fights, he had a reach advantage over his opponent. He also had blindingly fast hands and amazing footwork. He used these gifts to dance around the other fighter, peppering him with stinging jabs. When his foe tried to retaliate, he would simply dance back out of reach or bob his head. Eventually, most of his opponents grew frustrated. Then they got careless as they tried to chase after him. That gave Clay even more openings to land bigger punches.

Dundee used a mixture of flattery and encouragement to teach Clay. "I'm not his boss," Dundee said. "We're a team. We work together and I know how to work with him."[15]

Dundee let Clay think everything was his idea. If Dundee wanted him to jab more, he would say, "Gee, your jab is really coming along. You're getting your left knee into it and really stopping him in his tracks." Sometimes, that might not have been the case at all. Clay would soon be doing things the way Dundee wanted, but he would think it was all his own idea.[16]

Clay later said: "Angelo Dundee was with me from my second professional fight. And no matter what happened after that, he was always my friend … He was there when I needed him, and he always treated me with respect."[17]

Just eight days after he arrived in Miami, Clay had his second professional fight. He beat Herb Siler in the fourth round.

In early 1961, Clay won three fights in just over a month. On January 17, his nineteenth birthday, he beat

Ali fights Argentinean boxer Alex Mitoff in 1971. Ali won with a total knockout (TKO) in the sixth round during this televised fight.

Tony Esperti in three rounds. He scored a technical knockout (TKO) because Esperti's left eye was badly cut. A TKO happens when the referee, fight doctor, or the boxer's handlers determine that a boxer is unable to continue. In his next fight, Clay knocked out Jim Robinson in just two minutes.

On February 21, Clay fought in his first main-event bout against seasoned veteran Donnie Fleeman. He proved no match for Clay. The referee stopped the fight in the seventh round.

Throughout the rest of 1961, Clay continued to win bouts. His reputation continued to grow. Still, Clay had not yet battled a top fighter. Then, on February 10, 1962, he fought contender Sonny Banks in the legendary Madison Square Garden in New York City. Clay delighted the New York media with his wit, earning nicknames such as "The Mighty Mouth" and "The Louisville Lip."

Clay predicted that Banks would fall in four rounds. In the third round, Clay was clowning around, his hands at his sides rather than guarding his head. Suddenly, Banks caught him with a left hand to the jaw. Down went Clay, much to the delight of the crowd. Clay bounced back up and finished the round. In the fourth round, Clay came out strong, knocking out Banks. "I told you," he gloated to reporters. "The man fell in four!"[18]

Over the next few months, Clay won four more fights, all by knockout or TKO. On November 15, he battled his former teacher, the forty-eight-year-old Archie Moore. Moore did not want to fight Clay. "I had to fight him for financial reasons," Moore said.[19]

Clay boldly predicted that he would knock Moore out in just four rounds. Then he went out and did it. Although

TRASH TALK

In April, Clay was back in Louisville, battling Lamar Clark, a boxer who had knocked out his last forty-five opponents. He predicted that he would knock out Clay, too. Clay made his own prediction. He promised that Clark would fall in just two rounds. Clay broke Clark's nose and knocked him down three times, scoring a second-round knockout. Thus began Clay's habit of predicting in which round he would win a fight. "I said he would fall in two and he did," Clay said. "I'll continue this approach to prove I'm great."[20]

Later that year, Clay met professional wrestler Gorgeous George, who was known for bragging about himself to build interest in his upcoming matches. George told Clay, "A lot of people will pay to see someone shut your mouth. So keep on bragging, keep on sassing, and always be outrageous."[21]

Many people found Clay's banter refreshing. Others found it annoying. Even Angelo Dundee sometimes grew weary of his fighter's bluster. "There is only one Cassius Clay," Dundee once said. "Thank God."[22]

Moore was well past his prime, people still respected him. By beating Moore, Clay gained more respect.

Throughout 1963, Clay kept moving up the heavyweight ranks. First he knocked out Charles Powell. Next he won a decision against Doug Jones. Next, Clay traveled to London to battle British heavyweight Henry Cooper. In the first three rounds, Clay danced around the slower Cooper, peppering him with punches and opening a large cut over his left eye. Then, in the fourth round, Cooper caught Clay flush on the jaw with a huge left hook. Clay fell back against the ropes and then to the mat. Then the bell rang, ending the round. Clay wobbled back to his corner.

Dundee knew his dazed fighter had only the one-minute break between rounds to recover. Could he do it? Here came one of the turning points in Clay's career. A loss would have set back his championship plans. But Dundee came up with a trick to gain his fighter precious extra time to recover.

Earlier, Clay's glove had been split. Dundee tugged at the split to make it bigger. Then he called the referee over. There was a delay as they searched for a replacement glove. "I don't know how much time that got us," Dundee later said. "Maybe a minute, but it was enough."[23]

Recovered, Clay roared out for the next round. He pummeled Cooper with heavy punches. Before the round ended, the referee stopped the bout. Clay had survived a difficult fight and remained undefeated. Now he demanded a bout with Sonny Liston for the heavyweight championship of the world.

3

The Greatest

No one thought Cassius Clay was ready for a title shot. Not other fighters. Not sports reporters. Not even his own management team. Only one person thought Clay could win, and that was Clay himself. He had set the goal of becoming the heavyweight champion of the world. Now just one person stood in his way—Sonny Liston. Clay was determined to take the championship belt from him.

SONNY LISTON

Sonny Liston's name sent shivers down the spine of most fighters. He was big. He was tough. He was mean. He possessed one of the hardest punches in the history of heavyweight boxing.

As a teenager, Liston spent time in prison for his role in several robberies. There his boxing talent was discovered by a Roman Catholic priest, and his skill helped earn him an early parole. By 1960, he was a top contender for the heavyweight crown.

In September 1962, Liston knocked out reigning champion Floyd Patterson in the first round. A rematch in July 1963 ended with the same result—Liston winning on a first-round knockout.

Clay attended the second Liston-Patterson fight. When it ended, he climbed into the ring and grabbed the microphone. "Liston is a tramp; I'm the champ," he yelled. "I want that big ugly bear … If I can't whip that bum, I'll leave the country."[1]

After that, a reporter asked Liston how long it would take him to beat Clay in a fight. "Two rounds," Liston responded. "One and a half to catch him, and a half round to lick him."[2]

Sonny Days for Clay

Finally, in November a contract for the fight was signed. The fight was scheduled for February 25, 1964, in Miami, Florida. Most experts believed that Liston would whip Clay. Some even worried about the young fighter's safety.

Boxing attorney Sol Silverman said, "The proposed Cassius Clay-Sonny Liston heavyweight title fight is a dangerous mismatch which could result in grave injury to the young challenger. Besides, not one former heavyweight champion among the eleven now living regards Clay as being ready for Liston."[3]

Even Clay's backers did not think he was ready to take on Liston. "Everyone predicted that Sonny Liston would destroy me," Clay later recalled. "But it's lack of faith that makes people afraid of meeting challenges, and I believed in myself."[4]

Clay trained hard, and he studied Liston's style. He also started running his mouth. "I figured Liston would get so mad that, when the fight came, he'd try to kill me and forget everything he knew about boxing."[5]

Clay even composed a poem titled "Song of Myself," predicting his victory over the champion. In it, he said that the ringside observers would witness "a total eclipse of the Sonny!"[6]

Liston, meanwhile, said his left fist would do his talking for him. "It's gonna go so far down his throat, it'll take a week for me to pull it out again," Liston said. Hype for the fight was building.[7]

Then something happened that threatened cancellation of the bout. Word spread that members of the Nation of Islam were spending time in Clay's training camp. Many viewed the group, also called the Black Muslims, as radical. The fight promoters feared that people would refuse to come to the fight if the Black Muslims were there.

Fight the Power

The early and mid-1960s marked the height of the civil rights movement in the United States. Leaders such as Reverend Martin Luther King Jr. led nonviolent marches to demand equal rights for African Americans.

Not everyone shared King's vision of nonviolent change. The Nation of Islam, led by Elijah Muhammad, believed in opposing white oppression by whatever means necessary, including violence.

The Nation of Islam's message of asserting the rights of black people struck a chord with Clay. He kept his interest quiet. He feared that if people thought he was involved with the Nation of Islam it would prevent him from getting a shot at the heavyweight title.

Ali and fellow black Muslims listen to Nation of Islam leader Elijah Muhammad speak in Chicago in 1966. Ali changed his name from Cassius Clay to demonstrate his new faith.

The assassination of President John F. Kennedy in November 1963 caused problems within the Nation of Islam. Kennedy was a strong supporter of civil rights. Still, Malcolm X, one of Elijah Muhammad's disciples, proclaimed that the Kennedy assassination was a case of "chickens coming home to roost." He meant that Kennedy had failed to stop the violence, which had rebounded on him.[8]

A nation in mourning did not appreciate these comments. Elijah Muhammad feared that such remarks would hurt the Nation of Islam movement. He ordered

Malcolm X not to speak in public for ninety days. The incident marked the beginning of a major split within the Nation of Islam.

In January 1964, Clay spoke at a Nation of Islam rally in New York City. His involvement drew news coverage. When Bill MacDonald, who was promoting the fight, learned of this, he threatened to cancel the bout.

To make matters even worse in MacDonald's eyes, Clay had invited Malcolm X to Miami while he trained. Clay and Malcolm X had become close friends. "In time, Malcolm became my spiritual adviser," Clay later said.

JOHN, PAUL, GEORGE, AND RINGO—AND CLAY

About a week before his first fight with Sonny Liston, Clay met the Beatles. The British musicians were in Miami to perform on *The Ed Sullivan Show* as part of their first visit to America. Clay was late, and the Beatles grew restless. But then Clay burst through the door and greeted them warmly. The Beatles and Clay, who would become two of the biggest pop culture icons of the 1960s, took an immediate liking to each other. They clowned around together, with the Beatles even climbing into the ring. Once there, they posed for a photo in which Clay appeared to be knocking all of them out with a single punch.

"Malcolm helped me focus on my strengths, and he strengthened my belief in myself."[9] Finally, Malcolm X agreed to leave town until the fight. MacDonald said the fight could proceed.

At the weigh-in before the fight, Clay acted like a crazy man. "Float like a butterfly, sting like a bee!" he shouted. Then he lunged as if to attack the champion. Liston looked at him, confused. He wondered if the challenger was really crazy.[10]

The doctor at the weigh-in found that Clay's pulse rate was 120 beats per minute, more than twice his normal rate. His blood pressure was 200 over 100, an alarmingly high rate. The doctor said. "This fighter is scared to death, and if his blood pressure is the same at fight time, it's all off."[11]

Clay insisted that it was all carefully planned, designed to throw Liston off his game. "The truth of the matter is I've rehearsed and planned every move I make that day," Clay said. Indeed, he was so relaxed after the weigh-in that he took a nap.[12]

Despite all the hype, many fans stayed away, thinking the fight would be a mismatch. However, many people across the country paid to watch the fight broadcast on a screen at a movie theater or other venue. Little did they realize that they were about to witness history.[13]

In the final moments before going out to meet Liston, Clay seemed wary. His water bottles were taped shut to prevent anyone from tampering with them. He feared that someone would try to drug him to make him lose the fight. He did not even fully trust his own trainer, Angelo Dundee, or his fight doctor, Ferdie Pacheco. "The only thing that could hurt me, I thought, was something coming through the water," he said.[14]

The fight itself was nearly as bizarre as the weigh-in. In the early rounds, Clay danced around the slower Liston, peppering him with sharp jabs that opened a cut under the champion's left eye.

At the end of the fourth round, Clay came back to the corner, and his eyes were burning. He couldn't see. There have been many theories about what happened. Some people think Liston's handlers put something on Liston's gloves to temporarily blind Clay. Others believe that the liniment Liston was using for his sore shoulder

Ali takes a break from training in 1964 to goof off with the Beatles, the famous British rock-and-roll band that was taking over the air waves that year.

or the ointment that Liston's cornermen used to stop the bleeding under his eye accidentally got into Clay's eyes during the clinches.

Dundee used the minute between rounds frantically trying to clear out Clay's eyes by sponging them with water. It didn't help. Clay instructed Dundee to stop the fight. How could he fight when he could barely see his opponent?

This single moment marked a turning point in Clay's career. If he quit, no matter how good the reason, it might be years before he got another title shot. "This is for the heavyweight championship; no one walks away from that," Dundee told him. "Get in there and run until your eyes clear up."[15]

As round five began, Clay could see only the blurred image of Liston. He used his long arms to keep the champion away. Realizing Clay could not see, Liston pushed forward. He swung heavy punches at the challenger's head and body. Some hit their mark, but most missed. By the end of the round Clay's vision had cleared.

Clay dominated the sixth round. He realized Liston was discouraged and worn out. He hit the champion with jabs, hooks, and uppercuts. Back on his stool in between rounds, Liston spit out his mouthpiece. He had had enough. He later claimed that his sore shoulder prevented him from punching effectively.

Clay immediately sprang to his feet, his arms raised over his head in victory. "I am the greatest!" he shouted to the throng of reporters. "Eat your words!" he told those who had doubted him.[16]

At the age of twenty-two, Muhammad Ali had reached his goal. He was heavyweight boxing champion of the world. He was the greatest.

4
The Legend Grows

Winning a boxing championship is one thing. Defending it is a completely different matter. When Cassius Clay beat Sonny Liston, few people thought he would hold the title for long. Most believed Liston would defeat Clay in a rematch. If not, someone else would take the crown from him. Few thought Clay was as talented as he claimed to be.

People didn't quite know what to think of the new champion. Some found him charming and funny. Others thought he was brash and arrogant. But as his new religion became more widely known, public opinion turned firmly against him.

Two days after the fight, Clay made his religious views clear at a press conference: "Islam is a religion and there are 750 million people all over the world who believe in it, and I'm one of them."[1]

Meanwhile, the rift between Elijah Muhammad and Malcolm X had grown worse, splintering the Nation of Islam. Soon Ali was forced to make a choice between two men he greatly admired. Malcolm X was his mentor and friend. Elijah Muhammad was the leader of the Nation of Islam. In the end, Ali chose to follow Elijah Muhammad.

On May 14, 1964, Ali left on a month-long trip to Ghana, Nigeria, and Egypt. The people greeted him as a

A new Muslim, Ali joins other believers in prayer at a mosque during a visit to Cairo, Egypt.

hero. While in Ghana, his path crossed that of Malcolm X. Ali rejected his former friend, saying, "You left the honorable Elijah Muhammad. That was the wrong thing to do, Brother Malcolm." Then he turned and walked away from his former spiritual mentor.[2]

This decision haunted Ali in later years. "Turning my back on Malcolm was one of the mistakes that I regret most in my life," he later said. "I wish I'd been able to tell Malcolm I was sorry, that he was right about so many things."[3]

Several key things happened upon Ali's return. Herbert Muhammad, a son of Elijah Muhammad, became part of

A NEW NAME

Elijah Muhammad gave Clay a new name: Muhammad Ali. In Arabic, "Muhammad" means "worthy of all praises" and "Ali" means "most high." Neither of them could have known at the time just how appropriate that name would prove to be. At first, some sports writers refused to use the new name. Even the Reverend Dr. Martin Luther King Jr. disagreed with Ali's decision to join the Black Muslims and be renamed. King felt that the Black Muslims stood for racial segregation, and that this went against the racial unity that King sought.

his entourage. He introduced Ali to Sonji Roi. For all his brashness regarding his boxing skills, Ali was shy around women. He immediately fell for the lively Roi. According to her, he asked her to marry him on their first date. "I wanted to be his wife and his best friend," she later said.[4]

Although he had introduced the two, Herbert Muhammad did not think Ali should marry Roi. He feared she would tempt him from the strict religious path of Islam. Members of the Nation of Islam did not drink. They did not smoke. They did not wear flashy clothes. Muslim women were not supposed to wear makeup or short dresses.

Ali, however, was smitten. He and Roi married on August 14, 1964, just over a month after they first met. Soon after, he returned to Miami to train for his upcoming rematch with Sonny Liston. The fight was set for November 16 in Boston, Massachusetts.

Almost immediately, tension grew between Ali and his wife. "She wore lipstick; she went into bars; she dressed in clothes that were revealing and didn't look right," Ali later said. "She made vows, and then she broke them, and that brought on all sorts of quarreling."[5]

Sonji Ali denied that Ali's religion came between them, saying, "The problem was that certain people, not Muhammad but certain other people, couldn't control me the way they wanted to. It had to do with control."[6]

Back in the Ring

Over in Liston's camp, the former champion had no such distractions. He trained hard. He believed that he had simply taken Ali too lightly the first time. This time he would be ready. "Fight experts who saw him during this time said that they had never seen him look so good and be so ready," said Pacheco.[7]

Then, just a few days before the fight, Ali suffered severe stomach pains and vomiting. He was rushed to the hospital. Doctors found that he had a tear in his abdominal wall. The situation required immediate surgery. The rematch with Liston was rescheduled for May 25, 1965.

The delay hurt Liston more than Ali. Liston tried hard to keep his edge, but he was in his mid-thirties. At that age, a boxer's skills typically start to decline. Ali, meanwhile, was still in his early twenties. He continued to grow stronger. When he had healed from his operation, he began training again. As Pacheco put it, he

THE ASSASSINATION OF MALCOLM X

On February 21, 1965, a suspicious fire broke out in Ali's apartment in Chicago. While some suspected it might have been started because of Ali's identifying as Muslim, police ruled the fire an accident. Halfway across the country, Ali's former friend Malcolm X feared for his life. He believed the Nation of Islam was planning to kill him. On February 21, three gunmen murdered him as he gave a speech in New York. Although the gunmen were arrested, only one confessed to guilt, with the other two maintaining their innocence. No one knows if the one confessed attacker acted on his own volition or on the orders of someone within the Nation of Islam.

was "refreshed and recharged, enjoying the considerable attention he was getting."[8]

Once again, the political turmoil affected the Ali-Liston fight. The city of Boston no longer wished to host the bout. Instead, the small town of Lewiston, Maine, took on the event. All sorts of rumors swirled around the fight. One rumor said that followers of Malcolm X would try to kill Ali before or during the fight. Another rumor said that the Nation of Islam had convinced Liston to "throw" the fight, or let Ali win. But, despite the outcome of their previous fight, most believed Liston would win the rematch.

As the challenger, Liston entered the ring first. The small crowd booed as Ali came in. It seemed ironic that Liston, who had been so hated when he was champion, should now be the fan favorite. Jersey Joe Walcott, a former heavyweight champion himself, served as the referee.

The bell rang. Ali circled the ring clockwise, throwing left jabs and an occasional right. Liston tried to close in, but Ali moved too fast. Suddenly, less than two minutes into the fight, Ali caught Liston with a short, crisp right-

Ali stands over a fallen Sonny Liston, whom he knocked out during the first round of their May 1965 fight, allowing Ali to keep his title as heavyweight champion.

hand blow to the jaw. Liston crumpled to the canvas. The punch came so fast that few people even saw it.

Turmoil followed. When a fighter knocks down his opponent, he is supposed to immediately go to a neutral corner while the referee counts. If the count reaches ten before the fallen fighter gets up, the fight is over. Ali did not go to a neutral corner. He stood over Liston and yelled, "Get up and fight."[9]

After several seconds, Walcott finally managed to steer Ali away. Meanwhile, Liston rolled over and got to his knees, only to fall back down. The referee never did begin a count. Outside the ring, however, Nat Fleischer, publisher of *The Ring* magazine, was keeping count.

After seventeen seconds, Liston staggered to his feet. Walcott let the fight continue. Ali attacked again as Liston tried to cover up. Meanwhile, Fleischer was shouting, "It's over! He's out!" Walcott moved away from the fighters. He listened to what Fleischer was saying, then went back and stopped the fight. Ali raised his arms in victory.[10]

The controversy had just begun, however. People referred to the knockout blow as the "phantom punch." Some claimed that the fight was "fixed," meaning that someone had paid to determine the outcome. Others believed that Liston had been frightened by all the talk of a possible assassination at the fight. They thought he had taken a "dive," or simply pretended to be knocked out.

After the fight, Ali watched the replay of the fight on television. Even he didn't see the knockout blow. "I'm so fast, even I missed the punch on TV," he said.[11]

Later, Ali summed it up this way: "The punch jarred him. It was a good punch, but I didn't think I hit him so hard that he couldn't have gotten up."[12]

Still, many people saw the fight as a tainted victory for Ali. That belief, coupled with dislike and fear of the Nation of Islam, caused many people to hate Ali. But hating Ali and defeating him were two different things.

Fighting Dirty

Who could close the mouth of the boastful Ali? The next to try was former champion Floyd Patterson. At first glance, Patterson appeared an odd choice. Liston had knocked him out twice in the first round of their two bouts. Meanwhile, Ali had defeated Liston twice.

Still, experts remained divided about Ali's true ability. *Sports Illustrated* writer Tex Maule said that he "may be now—and certainly can be in time—the best heavyweight ever." But former heavyweight champion Joe Louis said that Ali "had a million dollars' worth of confidence and a dime's worth of courage … He's lucky there are no good fighters around."[13]

Ali and Patterson represented almost complete opposites. The press and public regarded the calm and polite Patterson as a gentleman. He fit the mold of what they thought a heavyweight champion should be. On the other hand, many black people were coming to see Ali as a hero. He believed in himself, and he wasn't afraid to speak out for his rights.

The prefight buildup took a nasty turn when Patterson made comments about Ali's religion and refused to call him by his Muslim name. "Cassius Clay is disgracing himself and the Negro race," he said. He promised to "reclaim the title for America."[14]

Muhammad Ali: Fighting as a Conscientious Objector

Ali took on Floyd Patterson on June 15, 1965. The two would fight again in November, with Ali beating Patterson after twelve rounds.

Ali responded by calling Patterson a "deaf-dumb Negro who needs a good spanking." Ali promised to deliver that spanking.[15]

The bout took place November 22, 1965, in Las Vegas, Nevada. Ali kept his promise, beating and humiliating Patterson. In the first round, Ali did not bother to throw a punch. He just kept making Patterson miss. Throughout the fight, Ali pounded Patterson. He knocked Patterson down in the sixth round, but Patterson rose before the count reached ten.

Several times, it appeared that Ali could have finished Patterson, but he seemed to ease off. Finally, in the twelfth round, referee Harry Krause stopped the fight. The crowd cheered the loser and booed the winner.

As 1965 ended, Ali sat atop the boxing world. Still, controversy continued to swirl around him. That was nothing compared to what would come next.

5
Living in Exile

In 1966 came a series of events that would change the course of Muhammad Ali's life. Some were personal. Others related to politics and religion. The biggest came when he chose to defy the US government and refuse to be inducted into the US armed forces. Standing up for what he believed would cost him his heavyweight title and millions of dollars. He did it anyway.

Ali's year began on a somber note as the courts granted him a divorce from his wife. She received an alimony settlement of $15,000 a year for ten years plus lawyers' fees. "I am the only one to beat him," she said. "He'll remember that for the next ten years while he's making my payments."[1]

Meanwhile, events taking place half a world away affected Ali's life as well. By the mid-1960s, the United States had become more and more involved in the Vietnam War. A Communist-backed regime ruled North Vietnam, and a pro-Western government controlled the South.

Insurgents known as the Vietcong sought to overthrow the government in South Vietnam and unify the country. The Vietcong were backed by Communist powers Russia and China. The United States feared the spread of

With recording artist Rozaa Rio (*left*), Ali holds up a newspaper displaying a headline about Vietnam War protesters, showing that he wasn't the only one who was anti-war.

Communism throughout Asia. Therefore, the goal was to keep Communism confined to North Vietnam.

By the end of 1965, nearly 200,000 American soldiers were stationed in Vietnam. To fill the need for soldiers, all American men over the age of eighteen were subject to being drafted.

At first, most Americans supported the war. Then, as casualties mounted, public opinion slowly began to turn. Eventually, the war polarized the nation. Many people, especially young adults who faced the chance of being drafted, opposed the war. Protests spread across college campuses and cities.

Some young men avoided the draft by going to college or getting married, both of which provided an exemption for service. Others joined the National Guard or the Peace Corps. Still others applied for status as "conscientious objectors." This meant that their religious beliefs prevented them from taking part in the war.

Like other young men, Ali had registered for the draft when he turned eighteen in 1960. Just before he became heavyweight champion in 1964, he took the qualifying examination. Some young men were rejected by the military for failing to meet physical, mental, or moral standards.

Ali passed the physical portion of the test easily but, as a poor reader, he struggled with the mental aptitude test. He especially struggled doing the word problems in math. "When I looked at a lot of the questions they had on them Army tests, I just didn't know the answers," he said.[2]

Ali's Army IQ score placed him in the sixteenth percentile of all those taking the test. At that time, the

THE VIETNAM WAR

Informal US involvement in Vietnam spanned twenty years, from 1955 to 1975. But in the mid 1960s, the number of US troops involved mushroomed. By the late 1960s, more than 500,000 US soldiers were serving in Vietnam. During the course of US involvement in the war, more than 47,000 troops died in combat. That ranks only behind the Civil War, World War I, and World War II in terms of casualties. The Vietnam War is also the second-longest US war of all time. It ranks only behind the Afghan War.

army did not admit anyone who scored below the thirtieth percentile. Concerned that he might not have been trying, the military retested him two months later, with three army psychologists supervising. Again he failed, and he was classified 1-Y, which meant that he was not qualified to serve.[3]

Some people thought Ali should have to serve despite his low score. Ali responded to the hoopla by saying, "I only said I was the greatest, not the smartest."[4] Still, he was embarrassed at being portrayed as stupid.

In early 1966, with the military needing more soldiers than ever, the mental aptitude percentile required for service was lowered from thirty to fifteen. Suddenly, Ali found himself eligible for the draft again.

On February 14, 1966, his lawyer requested deferment from military service for him. The request was denied, and Ali was reclassified 1-A, which meant he could be drafted at any moment. That day, he was flooded with calls from the media. Finally, when asked what he thought about the Vietcong, he answered in frustration, "Man, I ain't got no quarrel with them Vietcong."[5]

That statement further polarized public opinion about Ali. Many white people now viewed him as a draft dodger. Many black people, however, praised his courage in standing up to the white power structure. They felt the draft was unfair. Young black men were drafted in disproportionate numbers to young white men. Soon Ali became a symbol to the growing antiwar movement in general.

Taking a Stand Takes a Toll

The controversy threatened his next boxing match. He was scheduled to fight Ernie Terrell in Chicago, but the state's boxing commissioners ruled that the match could not take place in Illinois. They offered Ali a chance to "apologize" for his "unpatriotic comments," but he declined. "I'm not apologizing for nothing like that, because I don't have to."[6]

Promoters moved the bout to Toronto, Canada, but Terrell bowed out. Canadian heavyweight champion George Chuvalo took his place. Ali crushed Chuvalo, winning fourteen of the fifteen rounds on the judges' scorecards.

Not long before the fight, Ali applied for conscientious objector status on the grounds that going to war violated his beliefs as a Muslim. His request was denied. As part of the appeal process, he testified under oath, saying, "If it wasn't against my conscience to do it, I would easily do it. I wouldn't raise all this court stuff and I wouldn't go through all of this and lose the millions that I gave up and my image with the American public that I would say is completely dead and ruined because of us in here now."[7] In the end, Ali's request was denied.

That fall, Ali's contract with his Louisville management expired. He chose Herbert Muhammad, son of Elijah Muhammad, to become his manager. Because Herbert Muhammad represented the Nation of Islam, this turned even more people against the champion.

Most American cities remained unwilling to host an Ali boxing match, so his next three bouts took place in Europe. Over the next few months, he easily defeated Henry Cooper, Brian London, and Karl Mildenberger.

In November, he fought Cleveland Williams in the Houston Astrodome in front of more than 35,000 fans, the largest crowd ever to witness a boxing match indoors. Some experts believe this fight represented Ali at the very peak of his powers. He scored a technical knockout in just three rounds. According to some accounts, he hit Williams more than a hundred times in those three rounds. In return, he absorbed just three punches. He even unveiled the footwork that became known as the "Ali Shuffle."[8]

"That night, he was the most devastating fighter who ever lived," sports commentator Howard Cosell later recalled.[9]

On February 6, 1967, Ali returned to Houston for a bout against Ernie Terrell, a dangerous opponent who insisted on calling him Cassius Clay. Ali took his revenge in the ring by pummeling him mercilessly. He also

Ali and his brother, Rudy (*left*), sit and talk with the leader of the Nation of Islam, Elijah Muhammad Poole, in 1964.

taunted Terrell throughout the fight, demanding, "What's my name?"[10]

By the end of the fight, Terrell's face was badly swollen. Afterward, he required surgery on his damaged left eye. The vicious beating drew still more criticism for Ali. Some people believed that he held back from knocking Terrell out so he could dish out still more punishment. People also wondered how he could claim to be a conscientious objector to war and deliver such a vicious beating in the ring.

On March 22, Ali knocked out Zora Folley in the seventh round, leading Folley to call him the greatest fighter of all time. It turned out to be Ali's last fight for three and a half years.

Ali vs. America

On April 28, Ali reported as scheduled to the induction center in Houston. When his name was called as Cassius Clay, he refused to respond. At that point, Lieutenant Clarence Hartman of the US Navy took Ali to a back room and explained to him that refusing to be inducted was punishable by up to five years' imprisonment and a fine. Ali responded that he knew the consequences of his refusal.

Once again, Ali entered the induction room and his name was called. Again he refused to answer. He provided a written statement stating, "I refuse to be inducted into the armed forces of the United States because I claim to be exempt as a minister of the religion of Islam."[11]

Ali added, "I strongly object to the fact that so many newspapers have given the American public and the world the impression that I have only two alternatives in taking this stand—either I go to jail or go to the Army. There is another alternative, and that is justice."[12]

The New York State Athletic Commission immediately suspended Ali's boxing license and withdrew recognition of him as the world heavyweight champion. Other major athletic commissions soon followed suit. This made it nearly impossible for Ali to fight anywhere in the United States. Many people felt that this punishment was racially motivated. They believed that Ali would have been treated less harshly if he were white.

On May 8, Ali was indicted by a federal grand jury. The trial date was set for June, and he was released on bail. Prosecutors suggested that if Ali accepted induction, he could enter Special Services. This would allow him to fight in exhibition matches and entertain the troops rather than participate in combat. Ali refused.

Carl Walker was an African American lawyer who argued the prosecution's case against Ali. "The trial itself was cut and dried," he said. "Based on the law, the jury had to find him guilty."[13]

Judge Ingraham presided over the case. When the jury returned its verdict, Ingraham sentenced Ali to five years' imprisonment and a fine of ten thousand dollars—the maximum sentence allowable.

Ali's lawyers immediately filed an appeal, and he remained free from jail. However, Judge Ingraham ordered that Ali's passport be confiscated. State commissions prevented him from fighting in the United States. Without a passport, he could not fight abroad. In effect, he couldn't fight anywhere.

As his appeal slowly wound its way through the legal process, Ali's life went on. On August 17, 1967, he married seventeen-year-old Belinda Boyd of Chicago, Illinois.

He had met her during visits there on Nation of Islam business. Unlike his first wife, Belinda already observed the Muslim religion. She was quiet and preferred to remain in the background. "He was my first love," Belinda later recalled.[14]

In the years to come, the couple had four children: Maryum, twins Rasheeda and Jamillah, and Muhammad Junior. Ali loved his children, but he traveled so much that he was rarely around.

In December 1968, Ali served ten days in jail in Dade County, Florida, for driving without a valid license. "Little things you take for granted like sleeping good or walking down the street, you can't do them no more," he said. "A man's got to be real serious about what he

THE OLD COLLEGE TRY

Unable to box, Ali began giving lectures at college campuses. He spoke out on topics such as the war in Vietnam, being stripped of his boxing title, integration, and the notion of money versus principle. "They contained important insights that spoke to something deep inside me," he later said.[16] But though Ali was free to speak out against the US government, they were watching. All through his college speaking tour, Ali was surveilled by government agents, who filed reports on him after each speaking engagement.

Muhammad Ali: Fighting as a Conscientious Objector

believes to say he'll do that for five years, but I was ready if I had to go."[15]

Meanwhile, Ali's case worked its way throughout the courts. On May 6, 1968, his conviction was affirmed by the Fifth Circuit Court of Appeals. Ali was disappointed. Boxing was his life, and he hated being kept away from it.

Ali kept busy. He participated in a simulated bout against former heavyweight champion Rocky Marciano. Over three days, the two men filmed seventy-five one-minute rounds. There were a variety of different endings. In the United States, Marciano knocked Ali out in the thirteenth round. In England, Ali stopped Marciano on cuts.

Soon after, Ali appeared on Broadway in a musical called *Big Time Buck White*. His performance drew praise from theater critics. "He sings with a pleasant, slightly impersonal voice, acts without embarrassment, and moves with innate dignity," wrote critic Clive Barnes in *The New York Times*. "He does himself proud."[17]

Meanwhile, more people were coming to believe that the Vietnam War was wrong. They sympathized with Ali and others who refused to serve. "And, unlike most war protesters, Ali had at least put his money where his mouth was, a sacrifice that did not go unnoticed even among his critics," said writer Jack Cashill.[18]

"During his exile, Muhammad Ali grew larger than sports," wrote biographer Thomas Hauser. "He became a political and social force."[19]

Still, by early 1970 Ali had grown weary of battling the government. In May he announced that he was retiring from boxing. "I don't need no prestige at beating up nobody," he said. "I'm tired. And I want to be the first black champion that got out that didn't get whipped."[20]

Living in Exile

Ali and wife Belinda Boyd, along with their daughters, study a magazine featuring news about Ali, who can be seen on the back cover of the publication.

Then, on June 15, 1970, the US Supreme Court ruled that status as a conscientious objector could be allowed on religious grounds alone. This helped Ali's case. Although his specific case had not yet reached the Supreme Court, the ruling increased his chances for winning.

Ali's managers immediately wanted to put together a fight for him. Ali relented. He wanted to regain the crown he felt had been stolen from him.

Muhammad Ali: Fighting as a Conscientious Objector

Was he bitter about this part of his life, Ali was later asked? "I wasn't bitter at all," Ali replied. "I had a good time speaking at colleges and meeting the students."[21]

Some people suggested that he sue the boxing commission, but he declined. "Well, they only did what they thought was right … It's just too bad they didn't recognize that I was sincere in doing what I thought was right at the time."[22]

Some people, including former heavyweight champion Rocky Marciano, believed that Ali should not try to return to boxing. But Belinda Ali, who knew her husband best, responded. "He won it in the ring, and he'll lose it in the ring. That's the only way he'll give up his crown."[23]

Indeed, regaining his heavyweight title was more than just a goal for Muhammad Ali—it was a crusade for justice.

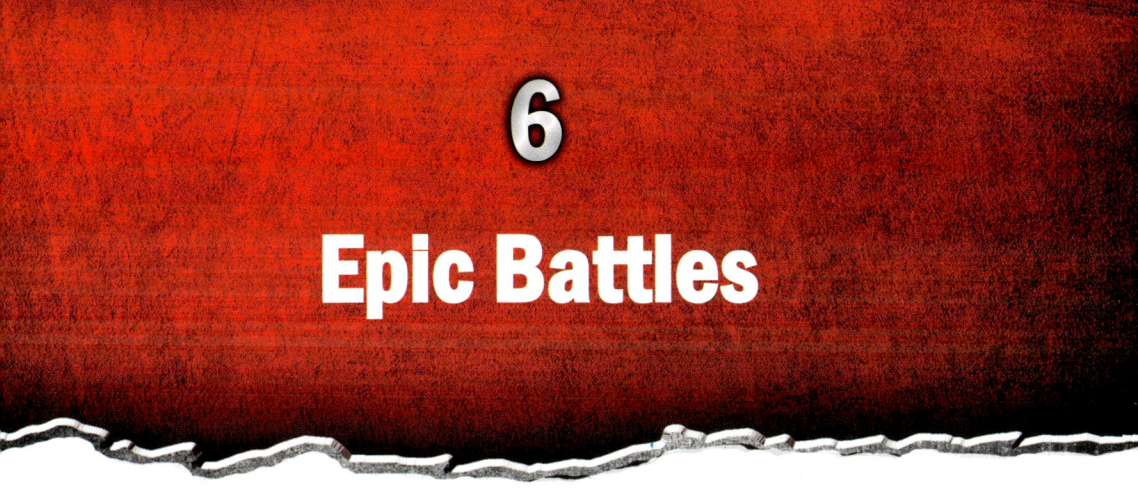

6

Epic Battles

Over the next few years, Ali would take part in some of history's greatest boxing matches. Those bouts would cement his legacy as the "Greatest of All Time." But first, he had to try to win back his title.

While Ali was in exile, the World Boxing Association held a tournament to determine his successor. Ironically, Jimmy Ellis emerged as the victor. As amateurs, Ellis and Ali had fought twice, splitting the two decisions. Ali looked forward to meeting Ellis a third time to earn back his heavyweight championship. Joe Frazier ruined those plans. On February 16, 1970, Frazier knocked out Ellis in the fifth round. As a result, everyone recognized Frazier as world champion—everyone except Muhammad Ali.

Getting Back in the Ring

Meanwhile, Ali's managers wanted him to box his way back into shape. They sought opponents they thought could push Ali—but not beat him. A bout with slow-footed but powerful Jerry Quarry fit the bill perfectly.

Promoter Bob Arum found it hard to find a site for the bout. Most states still refused to grant Ali a license to box. Finally, Atlanta, Georgia, offered to host the fight. The bout was scheduled for October 26, 1970.

Muhammad Ali: Fighting as a Conscientious Objector

Muhammad Ali and Joe Frazier (*left*) exchange some choice words during a press conference in 1970. The two would later take their fight to the ring to determine the rightful heavyweight champion.

Interest in the fight was tremendous. Many people, especially those in the black community, idolized Ali. They couldn't wait to see their hero in the ring again. Others still disliked Ali. Even many of these people, however, felt he should be allowed to fight.

How would Ali perform? He lost three and a half years from the prime of his career. Would he still be in shape? Did he still have his speed?

Ali realized just how important this fight was. "I'm not fightin' one man," he said. "I'm fightin' a lot of men, showin' 'em here is one man they couldn't defeat, couldn't conquer, one they didn't see get big and fat and flat on his back."[1]

A host of celebrities came to see Ali's return. And a grand return it was. In the third round, Ali opened a huge cut over Quarry's eye. The referee stopped the fight.

Just six weeks later, on December 7, Ali fought Oscar Bonavena in New York. The first fourteen rounds were fairly dull. But in the final round, Ali knocked Bonavena down three times and won the fight.

After this fight, the boxing world demanded a bout between Ali and Frazier. It was one of the most anticipated fights in boxing history. Both were former Olympic champions. Ali was undefeated as a professional. Frazier had won twenty-six fights in a row—twenty-three of them by knockout.

The two men also had totally opposite styles. That made the matchup even more intriguing. Ali liked to dance around his opponent and score with his long jab. Frazier, meanwhile, constantly pushed forward. He stalked his opponent until he saw an opening. Then he pounced, often with a devastating left hook. He did not mind taking three or four punches to set up one or two of his own.

As the bout drew close, excitement peaked. People everywhere talked about "The Fight." Each fighter received $2.5 million, a record purse.

This bout marked the first in a series of epic battles that Ali would fight against Frazier, Ken Norton, and George Foreman. These fights would cement his status as a boxing legend but take a tremendous toll on his body.

The fight took place on March 8, 1971, at Madison Square Garden in New York City. It was one of those rare sporting events that truly lived up to its hype. The fight seesawed back and forth. Ali won the early rounds, scoring with his jab as Frazier tried to move in close. But

THE GREAT DIVIDE

The Ali-Frazier fight divided fans. Most African Americans backed Ali, even though both fighters were black. Frazier was viewed as solid and dull. Ali was flamboyant and exciting. Furthermore, black America respected Ali for refusing to be drafted. Meanwhile, many white fans backed Frazier. They found him much more appealing than the brash Ali.

Ali fueled the fire by portraying himself as the champion of black people and Frazier as a tool of the white establishment. He said things like, "Any black person who's for Joe Frazier is a traitor."[2]

Ali said he was smarter and better looking than Frazier. Indeed, Ali claimed that he was the "prettiest" of any fighter because he was hit so rarely with strong punches from his opponents.

To Ali, this was all part of the act to stir up interest in the fight. Frazier, however, took the insults personally. He vowed to shut Ali's mouth by beating him in the ring.

Frazier kept up the pressure. In the middle rounds, he began to drive Ali into the ropes, where he battered Ali's body with heavy blows. This started to slow down Ali.

By the end of the tenth round, Frazier's face was puffed up and his eyes were closing. Yet he continued moving forward. In the eleventh round he rocked Ali with a left hook, but Ali managed to survive the round. At the end of round fourteen, most people thought the fight was very even. It seemed that the final three minutes would decide the fight.

In the decisive fifteenth round, Frazier knocked Ali down with a thunderous left hook. Ali quickly climbed to his feet, and the fight continued. Frazier won the decision in what came to be known as "The Fight of the Century." The battle left both fighters bloodied and bruised. Both had to go to the hospital once the fight ended.

Ali proved to be gracious in defeat. "Let the people who believe in me see that I'm not crushed, that I've had a defeat just as they have defeats, that I'll get up and come back again, just like other people do," he said.[3]

Ali wanted people to acknowledge the art and the science of his boxing. But, as Ferdie Pacheco noted, "what

Ali lands a left hook to Joe Frazier during their bout at New York City's Madison Square Garden in March 1971. Ali would go on to reclaim his title as heavyweight champion.

we remembered was his courage, his toughness, and his championship heart."[4] Meanwhile, Ali was already planning for a rematch.

Then, on June 28, 1971, exactly four years after Ali had refused to be inducted into the Army, the US Supreme Court reversed his conviction. With all charges against him dropped, Ali could now concentrate on regaining his heavyweight crown.

The King Reclaims His Crown

His next fight came on July 26, 1971, against his boyhood friend and former sparring partner, Jimmy Ellis. He knocked out Ellis in the twelfth round. Later that year he won a lopsided decision over Buster Mathis and a knockout victory over Jurgen Blin of West Germany.

In 1972, Ali fought often, defeating Mac Foster, George Chuvalo, Jerry Quarry in a rematch, and Al Lewis. That year, Ali also fulfilled a longtime dream by opening a training camp at Deer Lake, Pennsylvania. He built a gymnasium and cabins for his family and friends. One cabin was even used as a mosque.

Ali next hoped to schedule a rematch with Frazier. Those plans were derailed in January 1973 when George Foreman knocked Frazier out to win the championship. In February, Ali won a lackluster decision over Joe Bugner. Ali appeared for that bout attired in a robe inscribed "People's Choice"—a gift from singing legend Elvis Presley.

In March, Ali fought against a lightly regarded young heavyweight named Ken Norton. In the second round Norton caught Ali with a strong right. In Ali's corner at the end of the round, Dundee and Pacheco realized that

A SUPREME DECISION

In reversing Ali's conviction for refusing to be inducted into the army, the US Supreme Court noted there are three basic tests for granting conscientious objector status. First, the person must show that he is opposed to war in any form. Second, he must show that this opposition is based upon religious training and belief. Third, he must prove that his objection is sincere. The Court ruled 8–0 that Ali met these tests. One justice did not cast a vote. The Supreme Court limited its ruling to Ali's specific case. This prevented other Nation of Islam members from all claiming conscientious objector status.

their fighter's jaw was fractured. "Even after being told his jaw was broken, Ali emphatically refused to have the fight stopped," Pacheco recalled.[5]

The fight went twelve grueling rounds. Going into the final round, the bout was nearly even. Norton won the final round and the decision. Immediately after the fight, Ali had an operation to repair his broken jaw. The hardest part was that he had trouble talking for some time.

Those who disliked Ali delighted in seeing him defeated by a lesser fighter. Even some of his supporters thought the loss might mark the end of Ali's career.

"Losing to Norton was the end of the road, at least as far as I could see," said sportscaster Howard Cosell.[6]

Ali thought otherwise. And, oddly enough, his courage in continuing to fight despite his fractured jaw raised his esteem among many people. "In losing to Norton, he actually won," Pacheco said. "He won the respect of his boxing peers."[7]

They also saw Ali's gracious side. He refused to blame his defeat on his broken jaw. "Norton beat me today," Ali said. "Fair and square … Tomorrow, when I get well, I'll go out and whup [him], but today, Norton was the better man."[8]

It took Ali six months to recover before a rematch could be scheduled. This time Ali won a unanimous decision. His latest comeback was underway. He followed up just six weeks later with a win against Rudi Lubbers in a bout fought in Indonesia.

Then came Ali's rematch with Frazier. In the weeks leading up to the fight, Ali taunted Frazier, calling him "ignorant," which infuriated Frazier. The two nearly came to blows at an event with sportscaster Howard Cosell a few days before the actual fight. They were watching film of the first fight and commenting on it. Eventually, insults started flying. Frazier wrestled Ali to the floor. The two had to be separated.

Most viewers thought that Ali was playing around, as he often did. Cosell, however, realized that Frazier was not kidding. Cosell was genuinely scared, fearing that someone would get hurt.[9]

Ali dictated the pace of the actual fight. He won a unanimous decision. Frazier immediately demanded another rematch.

Rumble in the Jungle

In the meantime, Ali was on his way to one of the most spectacular fights of his entire career—a bout with George Foreman in the African nation of Zaire. This bout became known as "The Rumble in the Jungle."

Like Sonny Liston a decade earlier, many people considered Foreman unbeatable. He had won forty fights with no losses. All but three of the fights had ended in knockouts. "Sooner or later," wrote Dave Anderson of *The New York Times*, "the champion will land one of his sledgehammer punches, and for the first time in his career, Muhammad Ali will be counted out."[10]

Both fighters arrived early in Zaire to train. Ali continued to entertain people with his wit and his poetry. In one poem, he promised that he would once again "float like a butterfly, sting like a bee," adding that Foreman's "hands can't hit what his eyes can't see."[11]

The fight took place at 4 a.m. on October 30, 1974. The time difference allowed it to be seen in the evening in the United States. Sixty thousand screaming fans filled the stadium, almost all cheering for Ali.[12] Still, few experts believed Ali could stay with Foreman.

Ali realized he could no longer dance around the ring for the entire fight to avoid Foreman's powerful punches. Therefore, he unveiled a baffling new strategy. "What Ali did in the ring that night was truly inspired," said Ferdie Pacheco. "Ali figured out that the way to beat George Foreman was to let Foreman hit him."[13]

Basically, Ali's strategy consisted of leaning back against the ropes. Each round he covered up. Foreman flailed away, with Ali blocking most of the heavy blows. Sometimes Ali would launch a counterattack and pepper

Foreman with jabs. Still, it seemed certain Ali could not continue to absorb so many punches. Surely he must fall.

But Ali knew that Foreman had rarely fought more than a few rounds at a time. Usually he knocked out his opponents early in the bout. After the seventh round, Ali sensed that Foreman was running out of gas. But Ali was growing tired, too. He decided to try for a knockout. In the eighth round, the two fighters stood toe to toe. They traded heavy blows.

Then Ali caught Foreman with a strong right. The champion toppled to the canvas. Foreman struggled to his feet, but the count had reached ten. The fight was over. Ali's "rope a dope" strategy had worked.

Ali (*right*) takes on boxer George Foreman in 1974. The two fighters traveled to Zaire, in Africa, for the fight, which was dubbed "The Rumble in the Jungle."

"I take nothing away from George," Ali said after the bout. "He can still beat any man in the world. Except me."[14]

Once again, Ali reigned as champion of the world. *Sports Illustrated* named him Sportsman of the Year. President Gerald Ford invited him to White House. He seemed more popular than ever.

In March 1975, Ali easily defended his crown against Chuck Wepner, knocking out the challenger in the final round. But Wepner did knock Ali down in the ninth round. Ali said that Wepner was standing on his foot when he threw the punch, causing him to slip. Referee Tony Perez ruled it a knockdown, though.

That knockdown of a world-famous champion by a less-skilled fighter inspired a struggling actor named Sylvester Stallone. From that moment came the idea for the blockbuster series of *Rocky* movies. "Everybody wants a slice of immortality, whether it's for fifteen rounds in a fight or two minutes in their own life," Stallone said. "They want that sensation that they have a shot at the impossible dream, and that solidified the whole thing for me."[15]

Ali kept busy, defeating Ron Lyle and Joe Bugner. Those fights were just a prelude to the third Ali-Frazier bout, which remains one of the greatest fights of all time. Held in the Philippines, the fight was dubbed "The Thrilla in Manila."

The Thrilla in Manila

Ali faced a number of distractions. He didn't bring his wife to the Philippines. Instead, he brought a woman named Veronica Porsche. Tall and beautiful, Porsche had served as a poster girl for the Ali-Foreman fight. She traveled throughout the United States promoting the fight. She also went to Zaire. Ali was smitten with her beauty, and the two began an affair.

Ali took Porsche to a party at the presidential palace in Manila. The news soon got back to his wife, Belinda. She immediately flew to Manila. There she confronted her husband before flying home again.

Even as Ali's marriage crumbled, he continued to prepare for the big fight. As the fight neared, Ali taunted Frazier. One day at press conference, Ali pulled a black rubber gorilla out of his pocket and pounded it. Through it all, Frazier got madder and madder. He said nothing. He vowed to let his fists do the talking.

The fight was a classic. It was fought at 10:45 a.m. on October 1, 1975. That way it could be shown on closed-circuit television in the evening in the United States.

The fight seesawed back and forth. Ali won the early rounds, staggering Frazier several times. In the middle rounds, Frazier rocked Ali. But in the later rounds, Ali pummeled Frazier's face. Frazier's eyes swelled almost shut. By the end of the fourteenth round, he could barely see. His trainer, Eddie Futch, refused to let him come out for the final round.

Over in his corner, Ali could barely stand. He wasn't sure he could fight another round. He didn't have to. He had won.

After the fight, Ali attended a reception given by Ferdinand Marcos, the leader of the Philippines. He could barely eat or talk. "It was like death," Ali said. "Closest thing to dyin' that I know of."[16]

A few miles away, Frazier was in bed, trying to recover. "Man, I hit him with punches that'd bring down the walls of a city," he said. "Lawdy, Lawdy, he's a great champion."[17]

Years later, Ali would still cite that fight as a highlight of his career. Frazier "brought out the best in me, and the best fight we fought was in Manila," he said.[18]

Ali had regained his championship. He had won some of the most classic fights in history. He was arguably the most famous person in the entire world. What would he do next?

After his bruising battle in Manila, Ali chose an easier opponent. He knocked out Belgian champion Jean-Pierre Coopman is just five rounds. Next Ali battled Jimmy Young in what was supposed to be an easy bout. But Ali came in slow and overweight, and won a lackluster decision. Less than a month later, on May 24, 1976, he knocked out England's Richard Dunn in the fifth round.

Next, Ali faced a much tougher opponent, fighting Ken Norton for a third time. Like their first two battles, this one seesawed back and forth. Norton won the early rounds. Then Ali stormed back. Going into the final round the bout was nearly even. But Ali finished strong to win the decision.

Still, it was evident that Ali's skills were declining. He could no longer dance away from opponents' punches. He survived with strength, courage, and his ability to take heavy punches and battle back. But these epic bouts had all taken a toll on Ali's body.

Boxing is a young man's game, and the champion was growing older. Many people, even some of his friends and advisors, began to question whether he should retire while he was still on top of the world.

7
Falling Star

At his peak, Muhammad Ali seemed invincible. He believed he could win any fight, any time, against anybody. Unfortunately, he continued to believe that even as his body and skills began to erode. That proved to be devastating both to his career and his health.

Ali could have retired a hero after defeating George Foreman in Zaire. He could have retired a hero after beating Joe Frazier in "The Thrilla in Manila." He could have retired a hero after defeating Ken Norton in their third fight.

But Ali kept fighting. He waited more than seven months before climbing into the ring for his next bout. There he won a boring victory against the overmatched Alfredo Evangelista of Spain.

In 1975, Ali published his autobiography, *The Greatest: My Own Story*, coauthored with Richard Durham. The book was followed in 1977 by a movie titled *The Greatest*, which starred Ali. In general, the movie drew praise from viewers and critics alike.

On September 29, 1977, Ali stepped into the ring again for a bout against Earnie Shavers. With more than fifty wins, Shavers possessed one of the hardest punches in all of boxing. A sellout crowd packed Madison Square

Ali jokes around with photographers during promotion for his memoir, *The Greatest*, in 1975.

Garden. Another 70 million people watched the fight live on television.

Despite absorbing some hard blows, Ali was well ahead through most of the fight. Shavers came on strong toward the end. Some wondered if Ali would survive the final round. But Ali drew deep on his reserves and fought a masterful fifteenth round to secure the decision.

Teddy Brenner of Madison Square Garden thought Ali should retire after the Shavers fight. "The trick in boxing is to get out at the right time, and the fifteenth round last night was the right time for Ali," Brenner said. He backed that up by vowing that he would never again let Ali fight in Madison Square Garden.[1]

Fighting for His Life

After fights, boxers are required to give a urine specimen. This allows doctors to ensure that they haven't been taking performance-enhancing drugs. Ali's specimen following the Shavers fight showed no signs of drugs, but it did reveal something even more alarming—blood and entire sections of cells from tubules.

As Ferdie Pacheco, Ali's long-time fight doctor explained, "These cells filter the blood and make urine. They are not replaceable. They scar and impair kidney function." In short, their presence in his urine could indicate potentially serious kidney damage.[2]

Pacheco wrote a letter explaining the lab results and recommending that Ali not fight again. He sent copies to Ali, his wife, and three of his closest advisors. He did not

LIFE OUT OF THE RING

Ali was dealing with struggles outside the ring. In September 1976, Belinda Ali filed for divorce as Muhammad's affair with Veronica Porsche continued. "The whole time we were married, I tried to accept what he was about and what he liked," she later said. "And then everything got destroyed."[3]

On June 19, 1977, Ali married Veronica Porsche. They had lived together for some time and already had a ten-month-old child, Hana.

receive a single response. At that point, Pacheco left his role as Ali's doctor.

Ali wanted to keep fighting. His managers promised to find him "easy" fights. Soon they came up with an easy opponent who Ali really wanted to fight—Leon Spinks. Spinks had won an Olympic gold medal at the 1976 Olympics. Ali had beaten three Olympic gold-medal winners: Floyd Patterson, Joe Frazier, and George Foreman. He wanted to beat a fourth. Also, the inexperienced Spinks seemed like an easy target.

Ali didn't take the fight as seriously as he should have. He weighed 242 pounds (110 kilograms) when he began training, far above his ideal fighting weight. Furthermore, he sparred only twenty rounds before the bout.[4]

The fight itself, held on February 15, 1978, in Las Vegas, was dull. Ali spent much of the fight on the ropes, letting the awkward Spinks pummel his arms and body. Ali tried to rally in the last round, but it was too little, too late. Spinks won a split decision.

"Of all the fights I lost in boxing, losing to Spinks hurt the most," Ali said. "That's because it was my own fault. Leon fought clean; he did the best he could. But it was embarrassing that someone with so little fighting skills could beat me. I didn't train right."[5]

Ali demanded a rematch. The fight was scheduled for September 1978. This time Ali trained hard. He wanted the chance to become the first three-time champion of the world.

"I've worked this hard for a fight before, but never, never for this long," Ali told Pat Putnam of *Sports Illustrated*. "I hurt all over. I hate it, but I'm taking it. I know this is my last fight, and it's the last time I'll ever have to do it."[6]

Muhammad Ali: Fighting as a Conscientious Objector

Ali feigns sleep while playing with two of his daughters, nine-month-old Laila (*left*) and two-year-old Hana (*right*), in 1978. Laila would later become a boxer like her father.

The rematch took place on September 15, 1978, in New Orleans. The fight itself was lackluster, but the drama grew as millions of viewers around the world wondered if Ali could become champion for the third time. No fighter had ever done that. The crowd roared when Ali prevailed by unanimous decision. It was a fitting way to close what seemed to be the final chapter of Ali's remarkable boxing career.

Even Ali acknowledged that it was time to quit. "I'd be the biggest fool in the world to go out a loser after being the first three-time champ," he told one reporter.[7] On June 26, 1979, he announced his retirement from boxing.

In the meantime, he starred in a television miniseries called *Freedom Road*. Ali played the role of an ex-slave who fought in the Civil War and later became a US senator.

Soon after, Ali and Veronica moved to a mansion in Los Angeles. By this time, they had a second daughter, Laila, who was one year old. Ali's four children from his marriage to Belinda lived in Chicago with their grandparents. Ali had also fathered two other children outside of marriage while still married to Belinda.

Although the mansion seemed lavish, the quiet life bored Ali. He missed boxing. Part of the lure was money. Over the years, Ali had earned more in the ring than all the previous heavyweight champions combined. He had made millions more from various business ventures and endorsements. But Ali was incredibly generous, and much of his money was already gone.

Getting Back in the Ring

Eventually, Ali felt drawn back to boxing, where he truly felt comfortable. He missed the spotlight. In addition, he knew he could make millions by climbing back into the ring. In March 1980, he agreed to fight again.

Ali signed to fight reigning heavyweight champion Larry Holmes, who had been one of Ali's sparring partners in the 1970s. Ali received $8 million for the fight. Holmes, even as champion, received much less. Holmes did not want to fight Ali. He respected and loved the former champion. He was afraid he might hurt Ali.

Others were concerned about Ali's health as well. They noticed that he was speaking more slowly and softly. Prior to the fight, Ali underwent a two-day evaluation at the famed Mayo Clinic in Minnesota. He needed to do this in order to get his license for the fight. The report found "no specific finding that would prohibit him from engaging in further prize fights."[8]

Ali trained hard for the fight, but he was thirty-eight years old. He had lost much of his speed and his stamina. However, when he entered the ring he looked like the "old Ali." Some thought he could recapture the magic of years past. Holmes knew better: he crushed Ali that night. The fight was stopped after ten rounds. Holmes had won every round. Many people thought Holmes held back from trying to knock out Ali.

"Before the fight started, I thought I could win," Ali said after the fight. "But after the first round, I knew I was in trouble. I was tired, nothing left at all."[9]

For his part, Holmes said, "I'm prouder of sparring with him when he was young than I am of beating him when he was old."[10]

Despite everything, Ali planned to fight yet again. He couldn't bear the thought of ending his career on such a low note as the Holmes fight. He thought the thyroid medicine he was taking at the time was the reason he had

PAST THEIR PRIME

Elite athletes in many sports struggle with the decision of when to retire. Often, they believe they can excel for one more season or one more fight. Basketball legends Michael Jordan, Shaquille O'Neal, and Kobe Bryant all struggled in the final year of their pro careers. So did baseball superstar Willie Mays and NFL quarterback Brett Favre. Boxers face extra pressure to keep fighting because they earn so much money for a single bout. Other heavyweight boxers who fought well beyond their prime years include Larry Holmes and Mike Tyson.

performed so poorly. He wanted to make amends. A bout was set with Trevor Berbick for December 11, 1981, in the Bahamas.

Berbick won a unanimous decision in a lackluster battle. After the fight, Ali acknowledged that his boxing career was over for good. "I think I'm too old. I was slow. I was weak. Nothing but Father Time," he said. "I lost, but I lost honorably."[11]

Now it was time for Muhammad Ali to move on with the rest of his life. But he was destined to battle a foe more dangerous than any he had faced in the ring.

8
The Legend Lives On

Without boxing, Ali seemed lost and lonely. Friends also worried about his health. Even toward the end of his boxing career, his speech sometimes seemed slow and slurred. To many of his friends, the symptoms now seemed to be growing worse.

Ali tried to keep busy. He still traveled often. He spent more time with his children. He felt bad that his career had prevented him from being more involved in their lives. "Some of my children saw me more on television than in person, and spoke to me most often over the phone," he said. "I sincerely regret that loss to them and to me."[1]

But more time at home also created new stresses. Ali and Veronica began to argue. She wanted to pursue her own career, but Ali wanted her to remain at home. "I did adhere to a lot of his wishes," Veronica later said, "but it was pretty much an old-fashioned way of living."[2]

Meanwhile, Ali grew more and more worried about his health. He often felt tired. Sometimes his speech was slurred. He told his doctor that he was "walking like an old man."[3]

In 1985, while Western citizens were held hostage by terrorists in Beirut, Lebanon, Ali traveled to the Middle East in hopes of helping to secure the hostages' release.

Fighting a Losing Battle

In July 1982, Ali checked into the UCLA Medical Center. After a series of tests, doctors found no serious problems. Still he felt tired much of the time. On a trip back to Louisville, he had lunch with his old friend Yolanda "Lonnie" Williams. He had known Lonnie since 1962, when he was twenty and she was just five. Their families were neighbors in Louisville. She recalled that he was like a big brother to her when she was little.

Lonnie grew alarmed when she saw Ali. He stumbled and seemed depressed. After their lunch together, she made a life-changing decision. She decided to give up her career and move to Los Angeles. She got a condominium near Ali's mansion and began caring for him. "Muhammad took care of all my expenses," she said, "with Veronica's knowledge and consent. And I did everything I could for him."[4]

Still, Ali's health continued to decline. In September 1984, he checked into the Columbia-Presbyterian Medical Center in New York for a series of tests. "I'm not suffering," he told reporters, "I'm in no pain." Still, he was always tired, and his speech was slurred. "I'm not scared, but my family and friends are scared to death."[5]

Doctors concluded that Ali had symptoms of Parkinson's syndrome. "He's got a problem with his brain in terms of motor control," said neurologist Stanley Fahn of Columbia-Presbyterian. "We expect he'll respond to medication. After the medication, he should live as normal a life as possible."[6]

Symptoms of Parkinson's include shaking, slowness of movement, stiffness, and difficulty with balance. Other symptoms may include facial stiffness, a shuffling walk, and muffled speech. The disease typically worsens over time. Most people who have Parkinson's get it in their sixties or seventies. A few get it earlier. Head trauma, such as that suffered by boxers, can sometimes cause it.

In Ali's case, doctors at first thought that medication might relieve some of his symptoms. They stated that they did not believe his problems resulted from boxing.

Not everyone agreed with the diagnosis. Ali's longtime fight doctor, Ferdie Pacheco, maintained that at least some of Ali's problems were caused by blows absorbed in the ring. Over the years, Pacheco had seen many boxers exhibit symptoms of brain damage as a result of fighting. He saw many of the same symptoms in Ali. "Muhammad Ali progressed with shocking rapidity from boxing-induced neurological damage to a Parkinson-like symptomatology," Pacheco said.[7]

Indeed, over time his doctors came to the same conclusion. Years later, Dr. Stanley Fahn said that Ali had requested during his initial treatment that Fahn not state publicly what he thought caused his problems. But for Thomas Hauser's biography, Ali asked Fahn to speak freely. Fahn then said that he believed Ali's problem "was a post-traumatic Parkinsonism due to injuries from fighting."[8]

In addition to his declining health, Ali had to deal with the breakup of his third marriage. In September 1985, he and Veronica filed for divorce. The split was friendly. Still, Muhammad was sad to see the marriage ending and to realize that daughters Hana and Laila would be moving out, too.

The divorce became final in the summer of 1986, and Ali gave his ex-wife an extremely generous settlement. In the end, according to some sources, Veronica ended up coming out of the divorce with more money than her former husband.[9]

Not long after the divorce from Veronica, Ali asked Lonnie to marry him.

Almost from the time he married Lonnie, Ali's life started to improve. He was happy when he was with her. Also, his medical condition seemed to have stabilized somewhat. Soon the couple bought a farm in Berrien, Michigan. Ali loved life on the farm. He enjoyed bringing his family together there. "We would fly all of my children to the farm for summers," he said. "We called this time Camp Lonnie because she did all the work, organizing and keeping it interesting … Lonnie did it because she knew how much it meant to me."[10]

Ali adjusted to his new lifestyle and his physical limitations. He spent much of his time praying, studying the Qur'an, signing autographs, and entertaining the frequent visitors who came to the house.

Retirement

Ali's days at home revolved around a set routine. As a devout Muslim, he observed five prayer sessions daily, and he studied the Qur'an. He also spent a lot of time signing autographs. Indeed, it was said that he gave away more than one hundred thousand autographs a year.[11]

Ali appreciated the quiet of his farm. "Boxing was good to me while it lasted," he said, "but it was only a

While attending the Special Olympics in South Africa in 2003, Ali "fought" with Nobel Peace Prize winner and South African leader Nelson Mandela, who landed a "punch" on Ali's chin.

start to what I want to accomplish in life. Here on the farm, I can rest up for my true mission—loving people and spreading the word of God."[12]

Ali continued traveling. In 1990, he met Nelson Mandela, who had worked to end South Africa's apartheid, the system that kept whites and blacks separated and gave whites control of economic and political power. Mandela later became president of South Africa. Ali also met Mother Teresa, a Catholic nun who worked with poor and sick people in India. He became her friend. She took him to a hospital, where he visited with sick children.

During the 1990s, Ali's popularity continued to grow. In 1991, Thomas Hauser published his bestselling biography, *Muhammad Ali: His Life and Times*. It included interviews with some two hundred people, ranging from family members to boxers to notable people from around the world. The book brought Ali's life story to a whole new generation of people.

In 1992, a galaxy of stars joined in a television event to celebrate Ali's fiftieth birthday. Participants included actors such as Arnold Schwarzenegger, Sylvester Stallone, and Dustin Hoffman; singers Ella Fitzgerald, Little Richard, and Diana Ross; basketball star Magic Johnson; and sports commentator Howard Cosell.

Cosell was nearly as brash as Ali. The two had kidded each other for nearly three decades. On this occasion, however, Cosell offered solemn praise, noting that, "You are exactly who you said you are. You never wavered. You are free to be who you wanted to be. I love you." Ali was visibly moved as he listened to this tribute from his old friend.[13]

Despite his continuing health problems, the 1990s turned out to be a great decade for Ali in several ways.

For one thing, he and Lonnie adopted a little boy named Asaad. Ali doted on Asaad. He had always regretted not spending more time with his other children. He enjoyed having the chance for a fresh start with Asaad. He also maintained closer ties with his eight other children.

Also, the legend of Ali continued to grow. In 1996, millions of people around the world watched as Ali lit the Olympic flame for the Summer Olympics in Atlanta. The dramatic ceremony, which moved many to tears, reminded a generation of fans that Ali remained one of the most recognizable figures in the entire world.

LIGHTING THE OLYMPIC FLAME

No one knew who was going to light the flame to open the 1996 Summer Olympics in Atlanta, Georgia. Organizers kept it top secret. After other noted athletes brought the torch into Olympic Stadium and circled the track, former Olympic gold medal swimmer Janet Evans carried the torch up a long ramp. But who would actually light the flame? The crowd erupted when the spotlight showed Muhammad Ali standing at the top of the ramp. Many cried as Ali, his hand trembling from Parkinson's, lit the cauldron to open the Olympic games. Later, Ali told an interviewer how special it was to light the flame thirty-six years after winning his own Olympic gold medal.

That year also marked the release of *When We Were Kings*. This powerful documentary described the "Rumble in the Jungle" when Ali defeated George Foreman in Zaire. The film won an Academy Award for Best Documentary Feature. It also won legions of new fans for Ali.

Like Father, Like Daughter

In 1999, Ali learned that his youngest daughter, Laila Ali, wished to pursue a boxing career. At first, Ali expressed concern about her decision. She wondered if she would ever get his support. Finally he said, "Okay, come over here and show me your left jab." When she passed that test, she knew she had won him over.[14]

Laila Ali established a successful boxing career and became the most famous of her famous father's offspring. Like her father, she became a world boxing champion, retiring undefeated. She also became a noted actress.

Muhammad Ali took pride in Laila's achievements in the ring. But he also took pride in all his children.

> "The first 50 years of my life were a preparation for the next 50 years."
> — *Muhammad Ali*

Twenty-First Century Hero

In December 1999, Ali was named the athlete of the century by *Sports Illustrated* and the BBC. The new millennium brought even more honors. The highly acclaimed film *Ali*, starring Will Smith, was released in 2001. Smith earned an Academy Award nomination for his portrayal of Ali. Smith also earned even higher praise—approval from Ali himself.

In September 2000, the United Nations named Ali a Messenger of Peace. He is one of just a handful of world figures to have held this post. Messengers of Peace are high-profile people who agree to help focus worldwide attention on the work of the United Nations.

In that capacity and as a concerned citizen, Ali was involved in relief missions to countries in Africa, Asia, and the Caribbean. In 1998, he delivered medicine and medical equipment to Cuba. In 2002, he traveled to Afghanistan to raise awareness of the country's needs and the United Nations' work there.

Ali also worked to make life better for other boxers. In 2000, Congress passed the Muhammad Ali Boxing Reform Act. The act is designed to protect professional boxers by preventing exploitative, oppressive, and unethical business practices. It also called for assisting state boxing commissions in having better public oversight of the sport.

In addition, Ali has been involved in many other humanitarian projects. For example, his Celebrity Fight Night has raised more than $125 million for the Muhammad Ali Parkinson Center at Barrow Neurological Institute in Phoenix, Arizona. Leslie Chambers of the American Parkinson Disease Association said, "He brought the average American's attention to this disease. We're so grateful for him. In the long run, he's helped our community in a tremendous way."

In 2005, Ali received the prestigious Presidential Medal of Freedom. His citation read as follows: One of the greatest athletes of all time, Muhammad Ali produced some of America's most lasting sports memories, from

The Legend Lives On

In 2005, President George W. Bush presented Ali with the Presidential Medal of Freedom, the highest honor a civilian can receive from the United States.

winning the gold medal at the 1960 Summer Olympics to carrying the Olympic torch at the 1996 Summer Olympics. As the first three-time heavyweight boxing champion of the world, he thrilled, entertained, and inspired us. His deep commitment to equal justice and peace has touched people around the world. The United States honors Muhammad Ali for his lifetime of achievement and for his principled service to mankind.[15]

At the White House ceremony, President George W. Bush embraced Ali and pretended to box with him. Ali simply smiled.

Over the years, the effects of Parkinson's reduced Ali's ability to walk and to speak. Still, he kept busy, traveling as much as he could. He took special pride in his humanitarian work. The crowning jewel of this work is the Muhammad Ali Center, which opened in Louisville on November 19, 2005. Fans from around the world, including former US president Bill Clinton, attended the grand opening ceremony. "You thrilled us as a fighter and you inspired us even more as a force for peace and reconciliation, understanding and respect," Clinton said. "As your body slowed down, your heart speeded up."[16]

The museum features a variety of exhibitions reflecting Ali's six values: respect, confidence, conviction, dedication, giving, and spirituality. Interactive pavilions and multimedia presentations tell Ali's story. Visitors can try their hand at shadowboxing with the champ or

A HUGE INFLUENCE

Muhammad Ali's influence extended far beyond boxing. In the 1970s, he was arguably the most recognizable person on the planet. In fact, in 1999 *Time* magazine listed Ali among the 100 most important people of the 20th century. The list included politicians, scientists. entertainers, and others. That same year, the *Independent* newspaper of the United Kingdom ranked Ali as the top sports figure of the 20th century. The paper said Ali was the only person whose influence extended far beyond his own sport. In 2009, sports writer Mark Hauser ranked Ali sixth among the greatest, most well-rounded athletes of all time.

working on the speed bag in an exhibit that recreates Ali's Deer Lake Training Camp. They can relive the moment when Ali lit the Olympic flame in 1996 and see exhibits offering historical contexts for Ali's accomplishments.

After moving from their farm in Michigan, Ali and Lonnie spent most of their time in Arizona. They also owned a house in Jefferson County, Kentucky, near Ali's hometown of Louisville.

In September 2008, Louisville hosted the Ryder Cup, a golfing competition that matches a team of top golfers from Europe against a team from the United States. Before the matches began, Ali hosted a reception at the Muhammad Ali Center. Reporter Dave Perkins wrote, "Ali's entrance is one long standing ovation" as the crowd honors "the magnetic figure who changed the sports world, if not the world itself, more than 40 years ago."[17]

In his latter years, the man who once "shook up the world" with his brash ways prized the quiet things in life—his wife, his children and grandchildren, his religion. "My greatest accomplishments in life were achieved outside the ring," he said, "and my greatest privilege in life was becoming a messenger of peace and love. Because there is nothing as great as working for God."[18]

Conclusion

As Muhammad Ali grew frailer, his public appearances grew rarer. His last public appearance came in April 2016 at Celebrity Fight Night. He died on June 3, 2016 after a short illness, surrounded by his family. Ali's funeral took place in Louisville. Thousands lined the funeral route, tossing flowers at the hearse and scattering rose petals along the route.

At the service, former president Bill Clinton described Ali as a "free man of faith." Ali's longtime friend, comedian Billy Crystal, added, "Thirty-five years after he stopped fighting [Ali was] still the champion of the world. He was a tremendous bolt of lightning created by Mother Nature."

Muhammad Ali may be dead, but his legend lives on. At the height of his popularity in the 1970s, he was arguably the most famous person in the entire world. Even today, his name and face draw instant recognition almost anywhere.

During his years as a fighter—whether pummeling opponents in the ring or battling the establishment outside of it—Muhammad Ali seemed larger than life. Millions loved his brash personality and dazzling skills. Others resented his cockiness. But love him or hate him, he stirred emotions in people in a way that no one else could.

And where does Ali rank in the all-time annals of boxing? Ali's own heavyweight rankings of all time place himself first, Jack Johnson second, and Joe Louis in third place.[1]

In a 1998 ranking, *The Ring* magazine agreed, placing him atop the greatest heavyweights from all eras. ESPN.com named him the second greatest fighter in boxing history at any weight level, behind only Sugar Ray Robinson.[2]

Furthermore, Ali's longtime trainer, Angelo Dundee, reminds us that Ali lost three and a half of his prime boxing years while he was suspended from the sport for draft evasion. "We never saw him at his peak," Dundee says.[3]

"Muhammad is one of the few Americans, and certainly the first American athlete ever, to transcend the borders of this country and become an international

Mourners honor Ali with a Muslim prayer service, known as a Jenazah, after his death in 2016. He was later laid to rest at Cave Hill Cemetery in Louisville, Kentucky.

hero," noted sportswriter Bert Sugar. "He was the greatest sports hero of all time."[4]

But he was more than just a sports hero. The true magic of Ali is that his legend continued to grow even after he retired from boxing. His ongoing humanitarianism earned him accolades throughout the world.

After Ali's boxing career ended, Parkinson's ravaged his once magnificent body. His hands, once fast as lightning, now trembled. His once-slick speech was now slurred and slow. Oddly, his health struggles made him even more beloved. Even those who had not appreciated him as a fighter admired the grace and courage with which he now faced his physical challenges.

Bestselling author Alex Haley put it this way: "You know, there's a reality for anybody who studies history. And that is that ninety-nine-point-nine-nine-nine percent of the people who live will be totally forgotten a hundred years after they die. And of those who are remembered, only a small proportion will have made a significant and positive impact upon the world. But I think Ali will be one of those people."[5]

And how did Ali himself want to be remembered? "I would like to be remembered as a man who won the heavyweight title three times, who was humorous, and who treated everyone right. As a man who never looked down on those who looked up to him, and who helped as many people as he could. As a man who stood up for his beliefs no matter what. As a man who tried to unite all humankind through faith and love," he said. "And if all that's too much, then I guess I'd settle for being remembered only as a great boxer who became a leader and a champion of his people. And I wouldn't even mind if folks forgot how pretty I was."[6]

CHRONOLOGY

1942 Cassius Marcellus Clay Jr. is born on January 17 in Louisville, Kentucky.

1945 World War II ends.

1954 Begins taking boxing lessons after his bike is stolen; wins his first amateur bout.

1955 Wins novice boxing title in Louisville, Kentucky.

1959 Wins National AAU Light Heavyweight Championship for first of two consecutive years.

1960 Graduates high school near the bottom of his class; wins Olympic gold medal in light heavyweight division in Rome, Italy; wins first professional fight against Tunney Hunsaker; begins training with Angelo Dundee in Miami, Florida.

1961 Wins first main-event bout against Donnie Freeman; begins habit of predicting in which round he will win a fight.

1962 Fights for the first time in Madison Square Garden; defeats former heavyweight champion Archie Moore.

1963 Fights outside the United States for the first time, beating British heavyweight champion Henry Cooper; signs in November to meet Sonny Liston for the world heavyweight championship the following year.

1964 Defeats Sonny Liston to win the heavyweight crown on February 25; announces that he is a Muslim; takes new Muslim name of Muhammad Ali; makes a monthlong trip to Africa; marries Sonji Roi on August 14; signs for a rematch with

Muhammad Ali: Fighting as a Conscientious Objector

Sonny Liston, but the fight is postponed after Ali has emergency hernia surgery.

1965 Wins rematch with Sonny Liston on May 25 with a "phantom punch"; defeats former champion Floyd Patterson on November 22.

1966 Requests deferment from being drafted into the armed service for the Vietnam War, but the request is denied; divorces Sonji Roi; names Herbert Muhammad as his new manager; defends his crown several times.

1967 Refuses to be inducted into the US armed forces and is stripped of his boxing license and heavyweight championship; is indicted by a federal grand jury and is released on bail, pending appeal; marries seventeen-year-old Belinda Boyd on August 17.

1968 Welcomes birth of first child, daughter Maryum; loses appeal of his draft case in Appeals Court.

1969 Appears in the Broadway show *Big Time Buck White*.

1970 Welcomes twin daughters Rasheeda and Jamillah; US Supreme Court decrees that conscientious objector status can be allowed on religious grounds alone, which strengthens Ali's case and sets up his return to the ring; returns to the ring with victories against Jerry Quarry and Oscar Bonavena.

1971 Loses classic bout with Joe Frazier in March; wins Supreme Court ruling that causes all charges against him to be dropped; wins three matches on his comeback trail.

1972 Welcomes son Muhammad Jr.; fights six bouts

Chronology

during the course of the year, winning all six.

1973 Suffers a broken jaw and loses a fight against Ken Norton; wins rematch later in the year, along with two other bouts.

1974 Wins rematch with Joe Frazier; regains heavyweight title by beating George Foreman in the "Rumble in the Jungle" in Zaire; accepts invitation from President Gerald Ford to visit the White House.

1975 Successfully defends title four times, including "The Thrilla in Manila" over Joe Frazier; publishes autobiography, *The Greatest*.

1976 Welcomes arrival of daughter Hana, born to Ali's mistress, Veronica Porsche; successfully defends title four times, including a third bout with Ken Norton; battles to an embarrassing draw with professional wrestler Antonio Inoki in a boxing/wrestling match.

1977 Welcomes daughter Laila; divorces Belinda Ali and marries Veronica Porsche; successfully defends title twice, including a hard-fought bout against Earnie Shavers.

1978 Loses title to Leon Spinks and then regains it in a rematch, becoming the first three-time champion in history.

1979 Announces retirement from boxing; stars in television miniseries *Freedom Road*.

1980 Returns to boxing and loses badly to Larry Holmes.

1981 Loses final bout of his career to Trevor Berbick.

1984 Receives diagnosis of Parkinson's syndrome.

explaining the tremors, slurred speech, fatigue, and other symptoms he has been suffering.

1986 Divorces Veronica Porsche; marries Yolanda "Lonnie" Williams.

1990 Travels to Iraq on peace mission prior to the beginning of the Gulf War; succeeds in securing release of fifteen Americans held hostage in Iraq.

1992 Adopts son, Asaad.

1996 Lights Olympic flame at the Summer Olympics in Atlanta; enjoys release of *When We Were Kings*, Academy Award-winning documentary about the "Rumble in the Jungle."

1999 Watches daughter Laila begin a professional boxing career; is named athlete of the century by *Sports Illustrated* and the BBC.

2000 Is named a Messenger of Peace by the United Nations; celebrates passage by the US Congress of the Muhammad Ali Boxing Reform Act, designed to protect boxers from exploitation.

2001 Enjoys release of film biography *Ali*, starring Will Smith.

2005 Celebrates opening of Muhammad Ali Center in Louisville, Kentucky; receives Presidential Medal of Freedom from President George W. Bush.

2007 Celebrates sixty-fifth birthday; nominated for a Nobel Peace Prize.

2008 Attends the opening of the Ryder Cup golf competition in Louisville, inspiring both the American and European teams.

2016 Dies on June 3; thousands attend his funeral in Louisville.

Chapter Notes

Introduction

1. Thomas Hauser, *Muhammad Ali: His Life and Times* (New York: Simon & Schuster, 1991), p. 169.
2. Ibid., pp. 454–455.
3. Hauser, p. 203.
4. Ibid., p. 171.

Chapter 1: The Beginning of a Legend

1. Muhammad Ali with Richard Durham, *The Greatest: My Own Story* (New York, NY: Random House, 1975), p. 34.
2. Thomas Hauser, *Muhammad Ali: His Life and Times* (New York, NY: Simon & Schuster, 1991), p. 15.
3. Ibid., p. 16.
4. Hauser, pp. 14–15.
5. Muhammad Ali with Hana Yasmeen Ali, *The Soul of a Butterfly: Reflections on Life's Journey* (New York, NY: Simon & Schuster, 2004), pp. 5–6.
6. Hauser, p. 18.
7. Ali and Yasmeen Ali, p. 18.
8. Hauser, p. 18.
9. Ibid., p. 19,
10. Ibid., p. 19.
11. Felix Dennis and Don Atyeo, *Muhammad Ali: The Glory Years* (New York, NY: Hyperion, 2003), p. 32.
12. Hauser, p. 19.
13. John Stravinsky, *Muhammad Ali* (New York, NY: Park Lane Press, 1997), p. 14.
14. David Remnick, *King of the World* (New York, NY: Random House, 1998), p. 95.

15. Ali and Yasmeen Ali, p. 88.

16. Ibid., p. 28.

17. Hauser, p. 20.

18. Martin Kane, "Ready to Go in Rome," *Sports Illustrated*, August 29, 1960, p. 12.

Chapter 2: Golden Boy

1. David Maraniss, "When Worlds Collided," *Sports Illustrated*, May 27, 2008, p. 59.

2. Muhammad Ali with Hana Yasmeen Ali, *The Soul of a Butterfly: Reflections on Life's Journey* (New York, NY: Simon & Schuster, 2004), p. 34.

3. Thomas Hauser, *Muhammad Ali: His Life and Times* (New York, NY: Simon & Schuster, 1991), p. 26.

4. Felix Dennis and Don Atyeo, *Muhammad Ali: The Glory Years* (New York, NY: Hyperion, 2003), p. 44.

5. Maraniss, p. 60.

6. Muhammad Ali with Richard Durham, *The Greatest* (New York, NY: Random House, 1976), p. 70.

7. Ali and Yasmeen Ali, p. 40.

8. Ibid., pp. 30–31.

9. José Torres and Bert Randolph Sugar, *Sting Like a Bee: The Muhammad Ali Story* (New York, NY: Contemporary Books, 2002), p. 98.

10. Hauser, p. 31.

11. Stephen Brunt, *Facing Ali* (Guilford, CT: The Lyons Press, 2002), p. 22.

12. Dennis and Atyeo, p. 50.

13. Hauser, p. 34.

14. Ibid., p. 35.

15. Dennis and Atyeo, p. 54.

16. David Remnick, *King of the World* (New York, NY: Random House, 1998), 117.

17. Hauser, p. 36.

18. Dennis and Atyeo, p. 62.

19. Hauser, p. 49.

20. Dennis and Atyeo, p. 58.

21. John Capouya, "King Strut," *Sports Illustrated*, December 12, 2005, <http://vault.sportsillustrated.cnn.com/vault/article/magazine/MAG1114630/ index.htm> (September 15, 2008).

22. Hauser, p. 39.

23. Ibid., p. 54.

Chapter 3: The Greatest

1. Thomas Hauser, *Muhammad Ali: His Life and Times* (New York, NY: Simon & Schuster, 1991), p. 59

2. David Remnick, *King of the World* (New York, NY: Random House, 1998), p. 77.

3. José Torres and Bert Randolph Sugar, *Sting Like a Bee: The Muhammad Ali Story* (New York, NY: Contemporary Books/McGraw-Hill, 2002), p. 123.

4. Hauser, p. 60.

5. Ibid., p. 60.

6. Remnick, pp. 148–149.

7. Ibid., p. 147.

8. "God's Judgement of White America (The Chickens Come Home to Roost)" speech from December 4, 1963, Malcolm-x.org, <http://www.malcolm-x.org/ speeches/spc_120463.htm> (January 16, 2009).

9. Muhammad Ali with Hana Yasmeen Ali, *The Soul of a Butterfly: Reflections on Life's Journey* (New York, NY: Simon & Schuster, 2004), p. 76.

10. Muhammad Ali with Richard Durham, *The Greatest: My Own Story* (New York, NY: Random House, 1975), pp. 115–116.

11. Remnick, p. 181.

12. Ali and Durham, pp. 115–116.

13. Ibid., p. 117.

14. Ibid., p. 118.

15. Ferdie Pacheco, *Muhammad Ali: A View from the Corner* (New York, NY: Birch Lane Press/Carol Publishing Group, 1992), p. 78.

16. Remnick, p. 200.

Chapter 4: The Legend Grows

1. Thomas Hauser, *Muhammad Ali: His Life and Times* (New York, NY: Simon & Schuster, 1991), p. 82.

2. Jack Cashill, *Sucker Punch* (Nashville, TN: Nelson Current, 2006), p. 74.

3. Muhammad Ali with Hana Yasmeen Ali, *The Soul of a Butterfly: Reflections on Life's Journey* (New York, NY: Simon & Schuster, 2004), p. 85.

4. Hauser, p. 115.

5. Ibid., p. 129.

6. Ibid., p. 130.

7. Ferdie Pacheco, *Muhammad Ali: A View from the Corner* (New York, NY: Birch Lane Press/Carol Publishing Group, 1992), p. 81.

8. Ibid.

9. Muhammad Ali with Richard Durham, *The Greatest* (New York, NY: Random House, 1975), p. 122.

10. Hauser, p. 127.

11. Pacheco, p. 84.

12. Hauser, p. 127.

13. Hauser, p. 133. 14. Ibid., p. 139.

15. John Stravinsky, *Muhammad Ali: A Biography* (New York, NY: Park Lane Press/Random, 1997), p. 66.

Chapter 5: Living in Exile

1. Felix Dennis and Don Atyeo, *Muhammad Ali: The Glory Years* (New York, NY: Hyperion, 2003), p. 138.

2. José Torres and Bert Randolph Sugar, *Sting Like a Bee* (New York, NY: Contemporary Books/McGraw-Hill, 2002), p. 147.

3. Thomas Hauser, *Muhammad Ali: His Life and Times* (New York, NY: Simon & Schuster, 1991), p. 143.

4. Muhammad Ali with Richard Durham, *The Greatest: My Own Story* (New York, NY: Random House, 1975), p. 129.

5. Hauser, p. 145.

6. Torres, p. 151.

7. Hauser, p. 154.

8. Ann Oliver and Paul Simpson, eds., *The Rough Guide to Muhammad Ali* (London: Haymarket Customer Publishing, 2004), p. 48.

9. Hauser, p. 160.

10. Dennis and Atyeo, p. 150.

11. Hauser, p. 169.

12. John Stravinsky, *Muhammad Ali* (New York, NY: Park Lane Press/Random House, 1977), p. 81.

13. Hauser, p. 180.

14. Hauser, p. 184.

15. Ibid., p. 192.

16. Muhammad Ali with Hana Yasmeen Ali, *The Soul of a Butterfly: Reflections on Life's Journey* (New York, NY: Simon & Schuster, 2004), p. 98.

17. Ibid., p. 91.

18. Jack Cashill, *Sucker Punch* (Nashville, TN: Nelson Current), p. 118.

19. Hauser, p. 203.

20. Dennis and Atyeo, p. 160.

21. "Playboy Interview: Muhammad Ali." Reprinted in condensed form in *The Muhammad Ali Reader,* edited by Gerald Early (Hopewell, NJ: The Ecco Press, 1998), p. 154.

22. Ibid., p. 155.

23. Hauser, p. 207.

Chapter 6: Epic Battles

1. John Stravinsky, *Muhammad Ali* (New York, NY: Park Lane Press/Random House, 1997) p. 94.

2. Thomas Hauser, *Muhammad Ali: His Life and Times* (New York, NY: Simon & Schuster, 1991), p. 219.

3. Muhammad Ali with Richard Durham, *The Greatest: My Own Story* (New York, NY: Random House, 1975), p. 358.

4. Ferdie Pacheco, *Muhammad Ali: A View from the Corner* (New York, NY: Birch Lane Press/Carol Publishing Group, 1992), p. 106.

5. Pacheco, p. 111.

6. Hauser, p. 253.

7. Pacheco, p. 111.

8. Ibid, p. 115.

9. Ann Oliver and Paul Simpson, Editors, *The Rough Guide to Muhammad Ali* (New York, NY: Haymarket Customer Publishing, 2004), p. 69.

10. Hauser, p. 260.

11. Ibid., p. 269.

12. Ali and Durham, p. 400.

13. Hauser, p. 274.

14. Ali and Durham, p. 413.

15. Hauser, pp. 300–301.

16. Mark Kram, "Lawdy, Lawdy, He's Great," *Sports Illustrated*, October 13, 1975, p. 22.

17. Ibid., p. 22.

18. Hauser, p. 326.

Chapter 7: Falling Star

1. Thomas Hauser, *Muhammad Ali: His Life and Times* (New York, NY: Simon & Schuster, 1991), pp. 348–349.

2. Ferdie Pacheco, *Muhammad Ali: A View from the Corner* (New York, NY: Birch Lane Press/Carol Publishing Group, 1992), p. 151.

3. Hauser, p. 342.

4. Ann Oliver and Paul Simpson, eds., *The Rough Guide to Muhammad Ali* (New York, NY: Haymarket Customer Publishing, 2004), p. 164.

5. Hauser, p. 353.

6. Pat Putnam, "The Old Lion Eyes Leon," *Sports Illustrated*, September 11, 1978, p. 22.

7. Hauser, p. 361.

8. Ibid., p. 405.

9. Hauser, p. 412.

10. Ibid., pp. 412–413.

11. William Nack, "Not with a Bang but a Whisper," *Sports Illustrated*, December 21, 1981, p. 29.

Chapter 8: The Legend Lives On

1. Muhammad Ali with Hana Yasmeen Ali, *The Soul of Butterfly: Reflections on Life's Journey* (New York, NY: Simon & Schuster, 2004), p. 168.

2. Felix Dennis and Don Atyeo, *Muhammad Ali: The Glory Years* (New York, NY: Hyperion, 2003), p. 268.

3. Ibid., p. 268.

4. Thomas Hauser, *Muhammad Ali: His Life and Times* (New York, NY: Simon & Schuster, 1991), p. 469.

5. Ibid., p. 431.

6. AP report, "Neurologist Confirmed Ali's Damage in '80," Frederick, Maryland, News, September 21, <http://www.newspaperararchive.com> (September 16, 2008).

7. Ferdie Pacheco, *Muhammad Ali: A View from the Corner* (New York, NY: Birch Lane Press/Carol Publishing Group, 1992), p. 202.

8. Hauser, p. 492.

9. Dennis and Atyeo, p. 270.

10. Muhammad Ali with Hana Yasmeen Ali, p. 166.

11. Hauser, p. 484.

12. Ibid., p. 466.

13. "Muhammad Ali 50th Birthday Tribute with Howard Cosell," YouTube, n.d., <http://www.youtube.com/watch?v=ZsK8QU-EAWo> (September 10, 2008).

14. Laila Ali with David Ritz, *Reach: Finding Strength, Spirit, and Personal Power* (New York, NY: Hyperion, 2002), p. 142.

15. Citations for Recipients of the 2005 Presidential Medal of Honor, n.d., <http://www.whitehouse.gov/news/releases/2005/11/20051109-10.html> (September 15, 2008).

16. "Grand Opening for New Ali Centre," BBC Sport webpage, n.d., <http://news.bbc.co.uk/sport2/hi/boxing/4455412.stm> (September 10, 2008).

17. Dave Perkins, "In Louisville, They Adore Muhammad Ali," *Toronto Star*, September 18, 2008, <http://www.thestar.com/Sports/Golf/article/501564> (September 20, 2008).

18. Muhammad Ali with Hana Yasmeen Ali, p. 209.

Conclusion

1. Thomas Hauser, *Muhammad Ali: His Life and Times* (New York, NY: Simon & Schuster, 1991), p. 458.

2. Kleran Mulvaney, "How We Picked the 50 Greatest Fighters," ESPN, <http://sports.espn.go.com/sports/boxing/greatest/news/story?id=2815643> (January 16, 2009).

3. Hauser, p. 454.

4. Ibid., p. 452.

5. Ibid., p. 508.

6. Muhammad Ali with Hana Yasmeen Ali, *The Soul of a Butterfly: Reflections on Life's Journey* (New York, NY: Simon & Schuster, 2004), p. 205.

Glossary

abolitionist One who wishes to do away with something.

accolades Praise.

bout A contest or match, as in boxing.

brash Tactless or rash; it can also mean highly spirited in an irreverent way.

civil rights movement A movement in the United States to gain equal rights for African Americans.

confiscated Taken away, removed.

conscientious objector A person who refuses to serve in the armed forces for moral or religious reasons.

controversy A public dispute caused by a difference of opinion.

deferment A temporary exemption from being inducted into military service; deferments can be offered for a variety of reasons.

disproportionate Out of line with the proportion or number one would expect.

entourage A group of people who travel with someone of importance.

evasion The act of escaping, avoiding, or getting away from something or someone.

exile To expel or banish.

humanitarian Concerned with the welfare of the entire human race.

indicted Formally accused of a crime.

Glossary

inducted Admitted as a member; often used in connection with being taken into military service.

integration The act of mixing or bringing parts together as a whole; often used in connection with integrating races or religions.

knockout In boxing, a situation where a fighter is knocked down and cannot get back up by the count of ten.

mismatch In boxing, a bout in which one fighter is far superior to the other.

Parkinson's syndrome A set of symptoms similar to those of Parkinson's disease, which may include tremors, slurred speech, and lack of steadiness when walking.

poignant Affecting the emotions, often causing sadness.

prejudice Having an unfavorable opinion about someone or something that is not based on fact but on prior attitudes; prejudice often occurs based on race, religion, or national origin.

segregation The act of separating or keeping apart; especially used in the sense of keeping races separate.

separatism A belief in keeping people or groups separate from each other.

simulate To create a likeness or model of a situation or event.

surveillance The act of keeping watch over something or someone, often done secretly.

technical knockout A situation in boxing where the bout is stopped because a fighter is judged unable to continue by the referee, the attending physician, or the people in the boxer's corner.

transcend To go beyond.

Further Reading

Books

Ali, Muhammad, with Hana Yasmeen Ali. *The Soul of a Butterfly: Reflections on Life's Journey*. New York, NY: Simon and Schuster, 2004.

Ali, Muhammad, with Richard Durham. *The Greatest: My Own Story*. New York, NY: Random House, 1976.

Buckley, James, Jr. *Who Was Muhammad Ali?* New York, NY: Grosset & Dunlap, 2014.

Montville, Leigh. *Sting Like a Bee: Muhammad Ali vs. the United States of America, 1966–1971*. New York, NY: Doubleday, 2017.

Websites

Muhammad Ali Center

alicenter.org

A multicultural center dedicated to Muhammad Ali, the website features information on Ali's life as well as a multitude of cultural learning opportunities.

The Official Muhammad Ali Web Site

ali.com

The official website for Muhammad Ali features a full, interactive recounting of the boxer's life and struggles.

Films

Krantz, Les. *Muhammad Ali: The Man, the Moves, the Mouth*. Facts That Matter, 2012.

Lewins, Clare. *I Am Ali*. Universal Studios, 2014.

Mann, Michael. *Ali*. Sony Pictures, 2002.

INDEX

A

Ali, Laila, 77, 83, 87
Ali, Muhammad
   amateur boxing career, 16–21
   army classification, 49–50
   birth and childhood, 13–16
   children, 55, 77, 80, 83, 86, 87, 91
   conscientious objection to military service, 6, 8, 47, 49, 51, 53–54, 57
   death, 92
   divorces, 47, 74, 83
   heavyweight championships, 31–32, 35–37, 67–69, 77
   high school, 17–18
   legacy, 92–94
   lighting Olympic flame, 86, 89, 91
   marriages, 40–41, 54–55, 74, 83
   and Muslim religion, 8, 38, 40, 51, 84
   name change, 8, 40, 45
   Olympic gold medal, 19, 20–22, 23, 24, 86, 89
   Parkinson's syndrome, 82–83, 86, 89–90, 94
   retirement, 77, 79, 83–87
   surgeries, 41, 65

B

Banks, Sonny, 27
Black Muslims/Nation of Islam, 8, 32, 33–34, 38, 40, 42–43, 45, 51, 65
Boyd, Belinda, 54–55, 58, 69–70, 74, 77

C

Clay, Cassius, Sr., 13, 14–16, 18, 23
Clay, Odessa, 13, 14, 16, 23
Cosell, Howard, 52, 66, 85

D

Deer Lake Training Camp, 64, 91
draft, 8–9, 48, 49, 50, 62, 93
Dundee, Angelo, 9, 25–26, 28, 29, 35, 37, 64, 93

E

Ellis, Jimmy, 19, 59, 64

F

Foreman, George, 61, 64, 67–69, 70, 72, 75, 87
Frazier, Joe, 59, 61–64, 66, 69–71, 72, 75

G

Greatest, The, 24, 72

H
Holmes, Larry, 78–79

K
King, Martin Luther, Jr., 8, 32, 40

L
Liston, Sonny, 29, 30–32, 35–37, 38, 41–44, 45, 67
Louisville Sponsoring Group, 23–25, 51

M
Malcolm X, 33, 34, 35, 38–39, 42
Mandela, Nelson, 85
Marciano, Rocky, 56, 58
Martin, Joe, 11, 15–16
Moore, Archie, 24–25, 27, 29
Mother Teresa, 85
Muhammad Ali Boxing Reform Act, 88
Muhammad Ali Center, 90, 91
Muhammad Ali Parkinson Center, 88
Muhammad Ali: His Life and Times, 85
Muhammad, Elijah, 32–33, 38–40, 51
Muhammad, Herbert, 39, 40, 51

N
Norton, Ken, 61, 64–66, 71, 72

P
Pacheco, Ferdie, 35, 41, 63, 64–65, 66, 67, 74–75, 82–83
Patterson, Floyd, 31, 45–46, 75
Porsche, Veronica, 69–70, 74, 77, 80, 82, 83
Presidential Medal of Freedom, 88–89

Q
Quarry, Jerry, 59, 61, 64

R
Roi, Sonji, 40–41, 47
"Rumble in the Jungle," 67–69, 87

S
segregation, 11, 13, 24, 40
Spinks, Leon, 75

T
Terrell, Ernie, 50, 51, 52–53
"Thrilla in Manila," 69–71, 72

U
US Supreme Court, 10, 57, 64, 65

V
Vietnam War, 6, 8, 9, 47–49, 55, 56

WITHDRAWN